Thea Stilton

AND THE TREASURE SEEKERS

THE LEGEND OF THE MAZE

Scholastic Inc.

Library of Congress Cataloging-in-Publication Data available

ISBN 978-1-338-68722-4

Text by Thea Stilton
Original title *Tesori Perduti: Il Labirinto Incantato*
Art Director: Iacopo Bruno
Graphic Designer: Francesca Leoneschi / The WorldofDOT
Cover by Alessandro Muscillo and Christian Aliprandi
Illustrations by Giuseppe Facciotto, Chiara Balleello, Barbara Pellizzari, Valeria Brambilla, and Alessandro Muscillo
Graphics by Chiara Cebraro

Special thanks to Becky Herrick
Translated by Andrea Schaffer
Interior design by Becky James

10 9 8 7 6 5 4 3 2 1

Printed in China

First edition, October 2021

21 22 23 24 25

62

Dear friends,

Ever since we discovered the story of Aurora Beatrix Lane, the archaeologist who lived almost a century ago, our adventures have been full of excitement and mystery!

This time, we've just returned from a journey seeking one of the very precious ancient treasures Aurora found: the legendary Ring of True Love! To find such a treasure, our adventure couldn't have started from anywhere but the romantic city of Verona, Italy, the setting of Romeo and Juliet's tragic love story! From there, our voyage took us around the world — and ultimately to the secret base of our nemesis, Luke von Klawitz, in Alaska. It was full of so many traps and hidden dangers, we weren't sure if we'd make it out . . .

Join us on this new adventure!

Big hugs from the Thea Sisters,   PAULINA

nicky   Violet   Colette

PAMELA

AIRLINES

FLIGHT: B3754F
FROM: Mouseford Academy, Whale Island
TO: Verona, Italy

N° 036428

MEET THE THEA SISTERS!

Colette

She has a real passion for clothing and accessories, especially pink ones. When she is older she wants to be a fashion writer.

Paulina

She is generous and cheerful, and she loves traveling and meeting new people all over the world. She has a real knack for science and technology.

Violet

She loves reading and learning about new things. She likes classical music and dreams of becoming a famouse violinist!

Nicky

She comes from Australia and is passionate about sports, ecology, and nature. She loves the open air and is always on the move!

Pamela

She is a skilled mechanic: Give her a screwdriver and she can fix anything! She loves to cook. Her favorite food is pizza, and she would eat it every moment of every day if she could.

QUEEN OF MY HEART

Colette stepped onto the balcony and sighed. A movement below made her look down, and she saw two **LARGE BLUE EYES** staring up at her.

"Colette!"

"**YOU'RE HERE?**" she gasped with surprise.

"Yes! From the moment I saw you at the *dance*, you left a mark on my heart that I cannot erase!"

Colette blushed, but before she could reply, another squeak interjected.

"Coco, **hurry up**! We need to continue on the tour. There are other mice waiting to come in!"

Colette shook her snout, and the young ratlet with blue eyes vanished. Instead, her **energetic** friend Pam appeared, in the fur and whiskers.

"Okay, okay, I'm coming," Colette said with a sigh.

The visit to Juliet's balcony and the story of her sweet love for Romeo had dragged Colette into a romantic **daydream**, complete with a very charming suitor of her own!

Colette and the other Thea Sisters were in the city where **William Shakespeare's** famouse play took place: Verona.

And at that moment, they were actually

ROMEO AND JULIET

"With love's light wings did I o'erperch these walls,
For stony limits cannot hold love out,
And what love can do, that dares love attempt."

Romeo says these words in the second act of *Romeo and Juliet*, a celebrated play written by William Shakespeare at the end of the sixteenth century. The play tells the story of the love between two mice in Verona, Italy, who belonged to feuding families: the Montagues and the Capulets. Their love is deep and intense, but their story has a dramatic, tragic ending.

Similar stories of young love had been told many times throughout history, but Shakespeare's version was so moving that his work is still very famous today.

WILLIAM SHAKESPEARE

He was an English playwright and poet who lived from c. 1564 to 1616 and is considered one of the greatest writers of all time. He wrote 154 sonnets and thirty-seven plays that are studied and performed even today, five centuries later!

visiting a building known as Juliet's house! It even had a **balcony** just like the one where Romeo declared his love in the theatrical mousterpiece.

"So, what do you think of JULIET'S HOUSE?" asked Sebastiano, a ratlet the Thea Sisters had befriended. He was from Verona and had offered to be their **guide** to the area that weekend.

"It feels just like we're in the story!"

commented Nicky. "Thanks for bringing us!"

Paulina looked thoughtful. "**Shakespeare** was English,

so why did he choose to tell the story of a mouselet born in **ITALY**?" she asked.

Sebastiano smiled. "In Shakespeare's time, the story of young love was well known all across **Europe**."

"A very romantic legend," said Nicky.

Colette **sighed**. "And to think that Romeo and Juliet declared their great love right from this balcony . . . It must have been an **emotional** moment!"

It's a new addition!

"Coco, I don't want to spoil your cheese," Violet cut in, "but I read that that's not actually the case. Right, Sebastiano?"

Their friend nodded. "This balcony was an **ADDITION** built just last century. But the building itself is much older, and really belonged to the Dal Cappello family — a name that's similar to Capulet, **Juliet's** family in the story."

"That doesn't matter," Colette said dreamily. "Even if it isn't real, I want to believe it happened like Shakespeare described it! It's so romantic . . ."

Her friends smiled.

"Okay, sister, you can have your daydreams, if you like," Pam said, winking at Colette. "**But let's keep going!**" She headed toward the stairs that led up to the next floor.

A CLUE FROM THE PAST

Sebastiano continued guiding them through the building.

"The exhibition on this floor right now is a collection of **FEMALE CLOTHING** from Juliet's time!" he said.

In front of the mouselets were large glass cases full of long, luxurious dresses. They were made of **velvet** and other fine fabrics, and with lovely embroidery and sparkling jewels.

"*I can't believe how wonderful they are!*" Colette squealed, moving toward a case that held a pink ball gown with a pearl-covered bodice.

"Just think . . ." mused Colette. "Maybe

Juliet actually wore **THIS** to the ball where she met Romeo!"

Violet chuckled. "I don't think so . . . Juliet was just a charac —"

"Ohhh, don't spoil my fun!" Colette cut her off. "**Love needs imagination to live!** Imagine Juliet at the ball . . ." She began to dance around — until she lost her balance in the middle of a twirl and tripped over a **TILE** that was cracked.

Nicky sprang toward her. "Are you hurt?"

"Me, no . . . but the floor, yes," Colette responded, embarrassed. She looked at the tile that had JUMPED out of place. "We should call the attendant . . ."

"Maybe we can put it back ourselves," Paulina said. But when she picked it up to fix it, she SAW something very unexpected. On the back of the tile, in the corner, someone had engraved three letters.

Look!

"*ABL*," she whispered.

Nicky approached her. "What a strange coincidence! Those are the exact initials of . . ."

"*Aurora Beatrix Lane!*"

Pam finished her sentence. Aurora was an archaeologist and **EXPLORER** from the past, whose history the Thea Sisters had been passionately interested in.

Almost a century before, the intrepid Aurora had traveled the world looking for seven ancient and very precious hidden *treasures*. She wanted to bring them all to light so everyone could admire them — and at the same time, she wanted to keep them away from greedy collectors.

The five friends gathered to examine the tile. The pawwriting of the initials looked just like the pawwriting the mouselets knew well from Aurora's *letters* and **DiaRies** they had found.

"Could Aurora have come all the way here?" Nicky wondered.

"It seems that she went **ALL OVER THE WORLD!**"

Aurora Beatrix Lane

Colette responded. "But the real question is, why did she leave this **HERE**?"

"Maybe she found a treasure here in Verona?" Violet said.

The mouselets all exchanged a glance and crouched down on the floor to look at what was under the loose tile.

"There's a small space here," said Paulina. "But it's empty . . ."

"Of course — that would be too easy!" Colette replied.

"Um, excuse me." Sebastiano was standing above them. "Could you tell me what's happening? Who is Aurora?"

14

"She's . . . our friend," Pam explained hesitantly.

"And she traveled through here? Is she still in the area? You should ask her to join our tour!" Sebastiano said.

The mouselets LOOKED at one another, then burst into laughter.

"Well, it's not so simple!" began Colette. "But it's a long story . . ."

"And it would be better to explain it over a nice snack!" finished Pam. "Do you know of a place that might have some tasty treats?"

"A place?" the ratlet responded. "I know a ton of places! Come on, I have one in mind."

And so the group left Juliet's house and went back out onto the streets of Verona.

A NEW TREASURE

A few minutes later, the Thea Sisters and Sebastiano were sitting around a table at a **charming** café in the center of town. Pam was focused on their snack order.

"Can I suggest torta russa, or **Russian Cake**? It's a good one — despite the name, it is a typical dessert from Verona. It's made from puff pastry stuffed with amaretti cookies and almonds," he said.

"That sounds **delicious**! Russian cake for everyone, then!" Pam exclaimed. "And fruit **smoothies** and —"

"Pam, I think that's enough for now!" Nicky stopped her.

"Okay, okay, but if you end up still hungry,

don't take any of my cheese!"

They all **laughed**.

"Now, can you explain about this Aurora?" asked Sebastiano. "You've all been so **mysterious**!"

"Actually, her story is full of mysteries!" Violet said. "*Aurora Beatrix Lane* was brilliant and loved to travel. As soon as she was done with school, she dedicated herself to her passion: **archæology** . . . at least, until . . ." Violet stopped squeaking, uncertain.

"Until what?" asked Sebastiano.

Paulina answered, "On one of her first digs, Aurora found a **manuscript** that spoke of seven precious treasures hidden in different places around the world. Her gut told her that it was not just a **LEGEND**, so she went out searching for them . . ."

"Was she right? Did she find anything?" Sebastiano asked.

"Aurora *was* able to **FIND** them," Paulina responded. "But it wasn't so simple . . ."

Paulina continued. "The trouble for her began when she discovered that her professor **Jan von Klawitz** was also hunting for the seven treasures. But, unlike Aurora, who wanted to share the treasures with the world, he only wanted them for himself."

"How greedy!" the ratlet exclaimed.

The mouselets explained to Sebastiano how, thanks to the journals and the clues left by Aurora, they had been able to hunt down two of the seven precious treasures: the **ALABASTER GARDEN** and the **Queen's Jewel**.

"Wow!" Sebastiano cried, delighted by their story. "That's amazing!"

Colette smiled, then continued. "It feels like we're finally completing Aurora's **MISSION** by bringing these treasures to light."

Paulina nodded. Then she said to Sebastiano, "So you can understand our **SURPRISE** when we found Aurora's initials underneath the tile in Juliet's house!"

"Do you think it's a clue to finding another *treasure*?" he asked.

Nicky shrugged. "Who knows?" she said. "It could just be a sign that she visited this city."

"Or . . ." began Sebastiano, looking thoughtful. "Now that I think of it, there's a **LEGEND** that not many mice know, about a *Treasure of True Love* . . ."

"What is it?" asked Colette.

"Legend has it that it's an object with *great value* that belonged to Juliet," he replied. "They say that many adventurers have come to look for it, but no one knows anymore exactly what it is, or where it ended up."

Colette got excited. "It must be one of Aurora's seven precious treasures! We've got to —"

"**HOLD ON!**" said Pam. "We shouldn't rush to a conclusion."

"Is there anything else?" Paulina asked Sebastiano.

He shook his head. "No, I'm sorry . . ."

"But wait," said Paulina. "You said that not many mice know of this **LEGEND** How do *you* know it?"

The ratlet smiled. "Because of my great-grandfather! He was an archaeologist!"

"**LIKE AURORA!**" the mouselets exclaimed.

"Exactly!" Sebastiano said. "He had many colleagues around the world whom he shared research with. When I was little, I remember reading something about the famous *Treasure of True Love* in a letter . . ."

Colette clapped her paws. "Fabumouse!

Fabumouse!

All we have to do is read that letter, and we can begin to investigate the treasure of Verona!"

Sebastiano scratched his snout. "It might not be so simple. Like I said, I read the letter years ago, and now I don't know

22

exactly where to find it . . . But I can try. Actually, we can try together! Why don't you come over to my house now? We can look for the letter, and then I'll cook dinner. What do you say?"

"I say that's a mousetastic idea!" Pam exclaimed. "Even if we don't find the letter, we'll have delicious food to make up for it!"

The friends laughed and left the café to go to Sebastiano's house.

The breeze seemed to carry the scent of a new adventure. The Thea Sisters were ready for it!

PAGING THROUGH
MEMORIES

After a few minutes, Sebastiano stopped in front of a small WOODEN door in a charming redbrick building and announced, "This is it. Come on in!" He unlocked the door, and the group walked in and went up to the second floor to a small, well-decorated house.

"Wow!" Violet exclaimed, admiring a corner of the room completely covered by bookshelves packed with BOOKS. "You must **love** reading!"

Sebastiano smiled. "Oh yes, this is my parents' library! There are novels, opera librettos — which my **mom** loves — and even some books that belonged to my

grandparents." He opened a small **DOOR** in the lower corner of a bookshelf. "Here's where my parents keep all my great-grandfather Jacopo's things. It's mostly **PHOTOS**, books, and notebooks. When I was young, I loved to page through them and imagine his adventures. He was a hero to me!"

"Maybe we can find the letter that mentions the *Treasure of True Love* here," said Colette.

Sebastiano nodded. "It won't be easy, though. There is a lot in there, and it isn't very organized. But you're welcome to look through it . . . while I go into the kitchen to cook **dinner**!"

Pam followed him. "I'll help," she said. "I can't wait to learn some new recipes!"

The other THEA SISTERS sat down on

the floor and began to pass around the papers, starting with letters he'd saved that were sent to him by friends and colleagues. None, though, spoke of the treasure.

"**LOOK!**" Paulina said, and showed her friends a photo of a **young mouse** next to a Greek temple. "It's Jacopo at an excavation. Sebastiano looks a lot like him!"

"It's true!" Violet smiled as she paged through a notebook. It listed, in elegant pawwriting, the routes of many **trips** Jacopo had taken.

Jacopo, Sebastiano's
great-grandfather

"Athens, Rome, Turkey, Malaysia . . . Sebastiano's great-grandfather traveled a lot," Paulina said.

"Just like *Aurora*!" Violet said. "But there's no mention of the treasure . . ."

"Maybe not, but look at this!" Nicky squeaked eagerly. She passed the others an old book, a bit yellowed by time.

"It's an old book on **ancient Rome**," noted Violet.

"Yes, but . . . look at the inscription!"

On the first 🅟🅐🅖🅔 of the volume there were some lines written by paw:

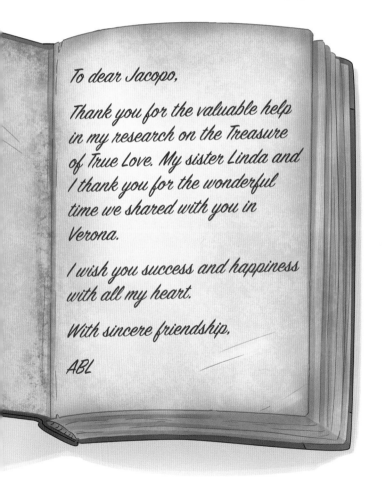

To dear Jacopo,

Thank you for the valuable help in my research on the Treasure of True Love. My sister Linda and I thank you for the wonderful time we shared with you in Verona.

I wish you success and happiness with all my heart.

With sincere friendship,

ABL

"Brie on a baguette! Aurora knew Sebastiano's great-grandfather?!" Colette said in amazement. "This is unbelievable!"

Drawn by the mouselet's squeaks, Pam and Sebastiano LOOKED in from the kitchen.

"Everything okay? Did you find something about the LEGEND?" he asked.

Colette spoke for everyone. "No, but we found something much better!"

On A New Trail

Pam had just served everyone **bigoli al pomodoro**, a pasta with tomato sauce (the local specialty), when Colette, Nicky, Violet, and Paulina showed her and Sebastiano the old book with the **dedication**.

"You didn't read about the treasure in a letter — you saw it in the dedication of this book!" Colette said.

The ratlet read it and gasped, "*ABL*?! You mean . . . ?"

Colette nodded. "Aurora Beatrix Lane

Bigoli al pomodoro

and your great-grandfather knew each other!"

"Extraordinary!" Sebastiano said. "Your beloved explorer and my dear great-grandfather crossed paths — because of Juliet's treasure!"

"Even if we don't know what this treasure is, now we know for sure that it exists, and that Aurora was on its trail," Violet said.

"In the dedication, she names one of her sisters, Linda," Paulina said. "So if she found it, did she give Linda its location?"

Sebastiano looked confused, and Nicky explained, "Every time Aurora found one of the seven treasures, she hid it and gave a clue to its location to one of her six sisters. She planned to go back for the treasures once she'd found all seven."

"Why hide them?" asked Sebastiano.

Paulina responded, "She wanted to keep them safe from her professor **Jan von Klawitz**, who wanted to steal them for his own private collection. Aurora planned to lend them to major museums so everyone could admire them."

"But she wasn't able to do it," added Colette with sadness in her squeak. "She

disappeared **mysteriously** in an aerial duel."

Silence fell over the room.

A moment later, Violet said, "But if *Aurora* did find the Treasure of True Love and told Linda where it was . . ."

"Then Luke von Klawitz must be after it!" Pam finished. She hurried to explain to Sebastiano, "He's a ruthless mouse who's trying to finish what his grandfather started."

"And we can't let that happen!" exclaimed Colette.

The mouselets smiled at one another. They'd already decided: They would investigate this new treasure! To begin, they had to research Linda's life and figure out if she had passed along any clues — or maybe even the treasure itself!

"We know from Aurora's inscription that Linda was in Verona," Paulina said. "If she lived here, we might be able to **track** her down somehow . . ."

"Maybe I can help you!" Sebastiano exclaimed. "But I'll tell you my idea tomorrow, because I need to hear from someone first. And also, I think that after this long day, we could all use a good night's rest!"

"I could not agree more!" Violet said before yawning.

They agreed to meet the next morning at nine. The Thea Sisters said good night to their friend and returned to their **hotel**.

SO MANY PAPERS!

The next morning, Sebastiano took his friends to a place in Verona that they would never have thought to visit: city hall!

"My cousin Guido works here," he explained. "He can **HELP** us find the archive of mice who have lived in Verona, where we can look for information about Aurora's sister!"

"**Cheese and crackers! Great idea!**" Pam exclaimed.

Guido kindly welcomed them into his office, a small room that he shared with two other colleagues. His desk was overflowing with **documents**, folders, files, and forms.

"Please excuse the mess," he said, moving

a few piles of papers. "What **EXACTLY** are you looking for? Sebastiano said something about a mouse who **MIGHT** have lived in Verona . . ."

"Yes — her name was Linda Lane, and she was British. She would have **come** here around a century ago," Violet explained.

"**A century ago . . .**" Guido said thoughtfully. He got up and went to a large cabinet that covered a wall of the office.

"To research so far back in time, we need to use the paper archive," he said.

Thanks for your help!

When he opened the cabinet doors, the mouselets' eyes widened: They had never seen so many papers crammed together! Where would they begin to **LOOK** in that sea of documents? Guido, though, seemed to know exactly where to put his **paws**. He soon gathered a dozen folders, which he placed on the desk.

"Okay — if this Linda ever lived in Verona, she'll be registered in here," he said.

The mice divided up the folders and began to examine their contents carefully. After a while, the friends began to lose hope . . . until Paulina exclaimed, "Here she is! It must be her! Linda Amaryllis Lane!"

Everyone instantly gathered around her. Guido looked at the paper and nodded. "This document says that she lived right

Here she is!

near here, in an area outside of the town center, toward the **HILLS** of Verona."

"What are we waiting for, sisters? Let's go!" cried Pam. Guido wrote down the **address** for them.

"This doesn't mean that you'll find anything," Sebastiano reminded them. "Or even that there's still a house there. We're talking about a long time ago . . ."

"You're right," Pam replied, "but I have a **hunch** that we'll find something. And there's only one way to find out . . ."

"Let's go see!" the Thea Sisters squeaked together. They thanked Guido and **RAN** out.

AT THE TOP OF THE HILL

The Thea Sisters enjoyed the view as Sebastiano drove the SUV out of the city. Their car **CLIMBED** up a road around the gentle hills on one side of Verona.

The **BRILLIANT** green slopes were largely covered with vineyards just showing their first clusters of grapes.

"Now I know why Linda chose to live here," Violet said. "It's so **beautiful**, it feels like we're in a painting!"

"Not to mention how well you eat here!" added Pam, munching on *risini*, a local specialty: pastries filled with custardy rice pudding.

Everyone **laughed**. "Pam, you never change. You're always thinking of food!"

Yum!

"Food is art, too!" she responded, pretending to be offended.

Before the friends could reply, Sebastiano slowed and announced, "We're here! This is the **address**!"

They were almost at the top of a hill, in front of a charming little house surrounded by **BUSHES** and flowers.

"There's still a house!" Colette said happily. "This is a good start!"

She rang the doorbell, full of hope. But no one answered.

Colette rang again. But again, no response.

"Too bad . . ." Sebastiano sighed,

disappointed. "I was beginning to think that we'd find another clue."

The friends were about to leave when an elderly rodent appeared through a doorway. She wore a

Good morning!

Oh!

large straw hat and held a basket of
FLOWERS.

Colette tried to find some resemblance
between the mouse and the photos she'd
seen of Linda, but she couldn't see any.

"Good morning!" the mouse said. "Are
you looking for someone?"

"Actually, yes . . ." Paulina answered. "But
we don't know if . . ."

"I know everyone
in this area!" the
mouse said with a
smile.

"We're looking for
someone who lived
here **a long time ago**,"
Paulina explained,
holding out a
PHOTO of Aurora

Aurora and Linda

and Linda. "This mouse on the right."

The elderly mouse studied the PICTURE. Suddenly, her face relaxed into an amazed expression and her eyes filled with **TEARS**.

"Signora Linda . . ." She sighed.

Colette took a step forward and put a paw on her arm. "So you knew her?"

"Yes, but I was very **young** . . ." Then she stopped and asked them, "And you all, how do you know her?"

"Well, it's a long story . . ." Colette said.

"In that case, come inside. We'll tell each other long stories over a nice **piece of cake**."

BRiLLiaNT iNTUiTiON

The mouse's name was Mia. She welcomed the Thea Sisters and Sebastiano into her living room and brought out a tray with fruit juice and a cake.

Then she began to tell her story. "When I first met Linda, I was not much more than a mouseling. I used to keep her company, and since she couldn't see very well, I would read her the travel books she loved. She'd never traveled much, but she liked hearing about **faraway countries**. I think it made her feel closer to Aurora . . ."

"Yes, Aurora traveled practically her whole life," Nicky said. "And we're trying to follow in her **pawsteps**."

Mia got up and fetched a wooden box.

"When Linda went back to England, she left me this house, and I've lived here since then. I keep my dearest mementos from long ago in this box," she said, and pulled out some old **photographs**.

You could see from the photos that Linda and Mia were very close friends. The Thea Sisters felt that they could trust Mia.

So they told her what they knew about Aurora, her search for the seven

Mia and Linda

treasures, and the conflict with Jan von Klawitz. And they filled her in on Jan's grandson, who was trying to complete Jan's selfish mission.

"Treasures . . . pursuits . . . now I understand why Linda was so worried about her sister," the elderly mouse said. "And now you're looking for clues to find this mysterious Treasure of True Love, right? I'm afraid I have nothing that could help you."

Violet glanced around the room and noticed a painting of a poetic Japanese landscape showing a large cherry tree in BLOOM.

The mouselet went up to the painting to admire it. It tilted a bit to the left, and Violet tried to straighten it out, but the FRAME kept slipping to the left.

"Oh, don't worry about that," Mia said. "I tried to **STRAIGHTEN** it every day for years, but it always tilts. I'm used to **seeing it** crooked!"

Curious, the Thea Sisters approached it.

"**HOW strange** . . ." Colette said. Turning to the elderly mouse, she asked, "Can we take it off the wall? Just to see what is behind it."

"Oh, sure! It's a painting that Linda put

up. **It's not valuable**, but she loved it."

"What are you thinking, Coco?" asked Paulina.

"It's only a hunch," Colette said, then took the canvas down and turned it over. The back was covered by a piece of brown paper.

"Maybe underneath . . ." muttered Colette. Then she raised a corner of the paper. On the lower right side of the frame, there was a bundle of envelopes tied with a ribbon! "Here's what made the painting **tilt**!" she said.

"What a good hunch, Colette!" Pam exclaimed.

A new little mystery was about to unfold . . .

DEAR AMARYLLIS

Colette placed the painting on the ground, took out the envelopes, and sat on the couch. She opened the first envelope **carefully** and pulled out a letter — and immediately recognized the pawwriting.

"They're *letters* between Aurora and Linda!" Colette cried.

Mia sat down by her. "Great Gouda! Those were there for years, and I never realized it!

"They probably have to do with one of the *treasures*, and Linda knew to keep it secret!" Colette said.

"She wanted to protect me," Mia agreed.

The mice began to read the first letter.

March 15

Dear Amaryllis (I love that your middle name is after that beautiful flower),

My heart is exploding with joy! I did it! I found the third lost treasure, the mythical Treasure of True Love!

I am so excited — it's the middle of the night right now, but I had to write you, even if by the light of a small, dim lamp . . .

I can't keep this joy to myself! You know that the search was long and difficult. But I never stopped, because I knew, deep in my heart, that this treasure really existed and wasn't just a legend.

So, after many mistakes and wrong turns, I discovered it in the most obvious place! Except I couldn't take it, because there was a familiar mouse on my heels: Professor von Klawitz.

I was too scared that he would follow me and steal the treasure, so I left it where it was. But I plan to go back and get it as soon as possible.

For now, it is safe, under a sliver of the floor in the house of the sun. I left my initials there.

Now I must go, because the light is fading and so is my strength. I'd better go to sleep and save energy for a new day of research . . . because there are still many treasures to find, and much work awaits me!

Your loving sister,
Aurora

"Now we're cooking with cheese!" Pam exclaimed. "Aurora said that she left the treasure in the 'house of the sun' . . . If we figure out where that is, we can go find it! Paulina, could you do a search on the **internet**?"

"Hold on, Pam!" Violet said. "I don't think the house of the sun is the actual name of a place. It has to be one of Aurora's puzzles!"

What does it mean?

Silence fell over the room. Then Colette exclaimed, "Aha! It's obvious!"

"What's obvious?" Paulina asked.

Her friend smiled. "This time, Aurora made her riddle based on a quote! And it's obviously from Shakespeare's **Romeo and Juliet**. There is a verse where Romeo, who is eagerly waiting underneath the window of his beloved, says, '*It is the east, and Juliet is the sun.*'"

Nicky jumped in. "So that means the 'house of the sun' is . . . Juliet's house!"

"And the 'sliver of the floor' where she left her initials was the TILE I tripped on!" Colette concluded.

"But there wasn't a treasure there!" Pam said unhappily.

"Let's try reading the last letter," said Colette. "I'm sure it will tell us something!"

June 9

Dear Amaryllis,

I'm writing you a few lines in a hurry. I must leave as soon as possible, to throw Jan von Klawitz off track.

My former professor won't let up, because he has lost this treasure, too. He wants to find me at any cost, to force me to reveal where I hid it.

Luckily, the Treasure of True Love is safe, thanks to you and our friend — it's secure in the shade of the cherry trees. There could be no better place for it.

When I find the right moment, I will go get it. I hope that day soon arrives . . .

For now, all I can do is send a hug and a hurried good-bye to you.

Yours,
Aurora

"Jan von Klawitz threw a wrench into the works again!" Sebastiano said **angrily**.

Colette nodded. "Aurora had to find a very secure hiding place for the treasure . . . **but where?**"

"'In the shade of the cherry trees' . . ." Nicky said thoughtfully. "Could this painting be a clue?" It featured a large cherry tree!

The mouselets examined the painting carefully but didn't find anything. Their investigation seemed to have hit a **DEAD END**.

FAMILY PASSIONS

Of course, the Thea Sisters weren't the only ones searching for the seven treasures.

Very far from Verona, in the cold expanse of Alaska, the heir of Professor **Jan von Klawitz** was in his secret bunker, sifting through the information he'd gathered.

"The next treasure will be mine. I will not let anything get in my way," Luke von Klawitz muttered. Especially not those squeaky little mouselets! He was in the control room, staring at a SCREEN that showed images of Verona, Italy.

While he concentrated on the aerial **P H O T O S** of the city, his wrist

Here I am!

communicator vibrated.

Luke answered the call and his assistant, **_Cassidy_**, appeared on the screen.

"Good morning, sir. I'm outside the base. Can you let me in?"

Luke replied in a dry tone, "Did you bring me something useful?"

She smiled and said, "Actually, I have something very interesting."

"In that case, come on in . . ." Luke grumbled.

Cassidy waited in the park above the hidden bunker.

Luke pressed some buttons on a special panel. In front of Cassidy, a square portion of the ground rose like a platform. When she climbed on the platform, it lowered, taking her directly into the **base**.

After a moment, Cassidy knocked on the control room door.

"**Come in!**" Luke said sharply. "I hope for your sake that you aren't wasting my time . . ."

"No, sir," Cassidy replied, smiling. "I must say I was very successful in this mission. Wait until you see what I found hidden in your ancestor Jan's house in London." She handed him a neatly wrapped package.

Luke unwrapped it to find an antique notebook. On its **cover**, elegantly pawwritten in blue ink, was: *JVK — Personal Notes*.

"I have reason to believe," Cassidy said,

"that this notebook has **information** that will be very useful for your research. Of course, I didn't open it, but —"

"That will do."

"**Wh·what?**" Cassidy stuttered in surprise.

Luke responded, "Your work is done for now. **Return** to the others and await my orders."

For you!

Hmm . . .

"But . . . since I brought you the journal I thought that we could at least read it togeth —"

Luke cut her off with a FIERY look. "I told you to go. Good day."

Cassidy sighed, then turned and left.

When he was alone again, Luke whispered, "Finally, it's just the two of us, Jan. I knew you'd hidden a record of your work somewhere . . . and I will use your words to complete your mission."

THEN HE OPENED IT.

Luke Von Klawitz muttered, "It's just like I thought! The Treasure of True Love was found in Verona!"

He pawed greedily through the notebook, looking for new clues to the treasure.

He read the next pages, then closed the notebook and sat quietly. He'd read that his

I can't believe Aurora got ahead of me again. She snatched the Treasure of True Love from my hands.

I was able to discover the location of the treasure: Juliet's house, in the city of Verona. But when I reached the hiding place . . . it was empty! Once again, that mouselet took the prize.

But now I know how she works. Aurora hides the treasure and leaves clues with an unsuspecting mouse. And I will comb the city to find whoever came into contact with the treasure. This time, I'll have the last word!

I was able to find a friend of Aurora's who she'd told about the treasure. The rat's name was Jacopo, and he's an archaeologist in Verona. He pretended not to know Aurora, but a source told me that they'd spent time together here in Verona.

Unfortunately, he doesn't know where the treasure is. When I asked him where it ended up, he mumbled something about cherry trees. Is it possible that Aurora buried the treasure in the roots of some cherry trees for some silly reason? I intend to find out . . .

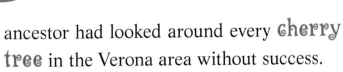

ancestor had looked around every **cherry tree** in the Verona area without success.

"Ha, ha, ha!" Luke burst out **laughing**.

Long ago . . .
Jan von Klawitz

Today . . .
Luke von Klawitz

"This time, you disappointed me, Jan . . . You underestimated little *Aurora*. But I won't make the same mistake: I already know where to look for Juliet's treasure!"

THE SECRET OF THE ALBUM

While the Thea Sisters and Sebastiano puzzled over the clue about the cherry trees, Mia began to **rummage** in an old wardrobe until she found a large volume.

"Here it is!" she said. "All this talk about dear Linda is making me miss her. I want to look at her photos!"

Colette went over and sat next to **Mia** on the couch.

"Sometimes it feels a bit lonely here," Mia said, opening the album.

Colette pointed at the first photo. "Here's Linda in front of an ancient **monument**!"

"That's the Arena," Mia said. "Have you been there?"

Sebastiano responded, "It was scheduled for yesterday, but then we **stumbled** onto Aurora's tracks, so —"

"Cheese niblets! You can't visit Verona and not see the ARENA!" Mia exclaimed. "It's an ancient Roman amphitheater that is extremely well preserved. You must go!"

"We should have time to check it out later," Colette assured her. Then she bent

Look at that!

over to look at another photo and exclaimed, "Look, Sebastiano! Here is your **great-grandfather** Jacopo!"

The ratlet peered at the photo. "You're right, it's him!"

Mia smiled. "Look what the city was like back then! There were very few cars." She paged through the **ALBUM**, and they saw photos of Linda in different places: at the movies; with an enormouse plate of pasta in

front of her; in a swimsuit by the water.

"Do you see the caption? Here she was on a trip to Lake Garda, a large lake nearby," Mia explained. "She was a really great **swimmer**!"

"Who is this other mouselet with her?" Colette asked, pointing at a young mouse standing next to Linda in a photo. They both were *smiling*.

"Ah, the young Kyoko Bianchi!" exclaimed

Linda and Kyoko

Mia. "I never met her. She went back to her home country a few years before I met Linda. Kyoko was one of her dearest friends — Linda spoke **HIGHLY** of her."

"And what is her home country?" asked Violet, curious.

"**JAPAN!**" Mia responded. "Her father was Italian and her mother was Japanese, and she mostly grew up in Japan. Linda had wanted to go visit her there at least once. I often heard her daydream about it: She really wanted to see the cherry trees blossom. But in the end, she never went."

"Cheese and crackers! Japan is the land of cherry trees!" Pam shouted.

"Yes, it's known for that, among other beauties . . . So what does that mean?" Mia asked, puzzled.

"The treasure is in the shade of the cherry

trees — what if Kyoko hid it in **JAPAN**?!"

That idea seemed to fill the room with a new light. The friends all spoke at once:

"How did we not think of it sooner?"

"It was right under our snouts!"

Hooray!

"Thank goodness you saved that **PHOTO**, Mia!" Nicky said. "You've been such a great help! Now we know where we need to go next!"

"I'm sure that Linda would be happy about that!" Mia smiled.

"One other thing . . ." Violet cut in. "Did Linda say what part of **JAPAN** her friend was from? Do you remember?"

Mia nodded. "I do. Kyoko Bianchi was from Tokyo."

A LITTLE DETOUR

After thanking Mia again and saying good-bye, Sebastiano dropped the THEA SISTERS off at their hotel.

"I'll pick you up when you're ready!" he said.

"*Thank you very much!*" Nicky squeaked, and the mouselets all scurried inside.

The Thea Sisters were in a hurry. They planned to pack their bags and get on the first flight to Tokyo to find the third treasure!

"I wish Sebastiano could **come with us** . . ." Colette sighed as she put yet another pink sweater in her suitcase.

"We'll send him lots of emails about what we find!" Paulina declared.

"I'm also sorry to leave Verona," Pam added. "But if it's to complete Aurora's mission, it's worth it!"

With their **suitcases** ready and their tickets purchased, the mouselets called their friend, who came to get them, as promised.

"We're a little bit early, but that's better than being late," said Colette.

"Tell the truth, Coco: You want time to go shopping in the airport!" Nicky teased.

"Who, me? No, no . . . I just LIKE being on time!"

Paulina cut in. "Sebastiano, are you sure this is the way to the **AIRPORT**? It seems like we're going into the city center!"

"You can't hide anything from the THEA SISTERS!" Sebastiano laughed. "Actually, since you have some time, I thought of a little detour . . ."

Then he **PARKED** in an alley and said, "You'll have to trust me — let's go!"

That was how the Thea Sisters found themselves in front of one of the most beautiful ancient **monuments** they'd ever seen. Two floors of perfect arches made up the outside of a majestic circular stone building.

"And here we are . . . the famouse Arena

You wanted to surprise us?

of Verona!" Sebastiano announced.

"Wow!" the mouselets exclaimed.

"So, what do you say, shall we take a tour?"

"Yes, please, with **cheese** on top!" Pam said.

The inside of the Arena was just as wonderful.

"Long ago, they held games and shows here. Today, it is still a fabumouse venue for concerts, operas, and plays!" Sebastiano explained.

"**HOW WONDERFUL!**" the mouselets said, admiring the huge circular space.

Very soon, though, it was time to leave.

"Sebastiano, thank you so much for this last **stop**," said Colette.

"I wanted to show you more of the city, but I understand that you have an important

MISSION to complete," he responded.

As the Thea Sisters headed into the airport, they called to him, "**Thank you** for everything! We'll let you know what happens!"

In the boarding area, Paulina pulled out her tablet. "While we wait for the flight, let's do some research on **KYOKO** and her family," she said.

"Great idea," Colette agreed. "*Treasure of True Love*, here we come!"

ON THE STREETS
OF TOKYO

Once they arrived at Narita Airport, the Thea Sisters took an express *train* to the center of Tokyo, Japan's capital and its largest city.

"The first address I found for a possible relative of Kyoko is in the **Shibuya** neighborhood," Paulina said, checking her notes on her tablet.

"Okay, then," Nicky said, looking at the railway **MAP**. "We should get off at the first stop!"

"Can't we go by the hotel first to drop off our luggage?" Colette asked.

Pam chuckled. "I told you it would be more comfortable to bring a **tiny** backpack

Huff, puff . . . and not a **GIGANTIC** one . . ."

"I brought only what I needed!" Colette replied, struggling with her big backpack.

"Here we are!" Violet interrupted, dragging them off the train before the doors closed again.

The **five friends** found themselves in a crowded station. Mice walked quickly in every direction.

"Great Gorgonzola! It seems that everyone has somewhere to be," Pam commented.

"We should hurry, too! This first **address** might not even be right," Paulina replied. "Assuming we find it . . .

The GPS on my tablet is not very clear. I think it's that way . . ."

The mouselets started down one street, but after a half block, the **navigator** began to reroute them.

"Oh no! We're going in the wrong **direction**," Nicky said. "We should've turned **LEFT**!"

"Left?! It seemed to me that we should go this way —"

"No, let's try that way!"

The friends, more and more **confused**, wandered around a tangle of streets that were dotted with tall buildings and mega-screens. Eventually, Paulina lowered her tablet unhappily.

The mice realized they had reached a huge crosswalk, so wide that the **VIEW** was lost in a sea of mice hurrying past.

"Cheese niblets! I read about this crosswalk: It's the biggest in the world!" Violet cried. "I think I know where we are! Let me see the **MAP** . . ."

Finally, the mouselets found the address they were looking for. It was a tall **SKYSCRAPER**, like many others in that area of the city.

The friends entered the building and went up to the reception desk.

"Excuse me, we're looking for **Amrita Bianchi**," Colette said.

The doormouse picked up a phone and said something in Japanese to the mouse on the other end, then turned to the Thea Sisters. "She's waiting for you on the twenty-second floor, apartment **SEVENTEEN**."

"You mean we have to go up twenty-two floors inside that tiny elevator?" Nicky said, worried. She couldn't stand small spaces.

"You can do it!" Paulina said. "Just think, soon, we could discover something about Aurora's treasure!"

After a quick ride, the mice stepped out into a long corridor. The door to apartment number 17 opened to a smiling mouselet.

"Do you like my fur?" Amrita Bianchi asked with a big smile. "It took almost two hours to get it this way!"

Then she began to laugh, enjoying the astonished faces of the Thea Sisters. "Ha, ha, ha! I guess you've never seen a COSPLAYER!"

Pam asked, "COS . . . what?"

"Cosplayer," Amrita said. "It comes from the words *costume play* — it's someone who dresses up as a fictional character from a book, comic, or movie!"

"Well, your COSTUME is gorgeous!" Colette commented.

"Thanks! I thought you were some friends I have been waiting for," Amrita said. "Were you looking for me?"

The Thea Sisters explained that they were looking for descendants of Kyoko Bianchi, who'd lived two or three generations before.

"I don't know that name," the mouselet said. "I'm sorry."

Just then the elevator OPENED and three

Come with us?

young rodents came out. They were dressed like Amrita.

"Here are my friends!" Amrita said. "Hey, do you want to come out with us?"

"Thank you, but we still have work to do," Paulina said.

Thanks, but we can't!

ACCIDENTAL SINGERS

The Thea Sisters **REACHED** the second and last address of a possible relative of Kyoko: a mouse named Shinobu Bianchi, who lived in the Shinjuku neighborhood.

"We're here," said Paulina in front of a **small** one-story house. "All we have to do is ri —"

Just then a ratlet **RUSHED** out the door, almost knocking Paulina over.

"Oh, pardon me!" the stranger excused

Oh!

himself. "I'm RUNNING to work — I'm late, and I didn't see you . . ."

"It's okay!" said Paulina. "Could you tell us if Shinobu Bianchi lives here?"

The mouse was startled. "That's me! Why?"

"We have a few questions for you," Colette responded. "It won't take long . . ."

"I'm sorry, but I really don't have time!" he said. "Why don't you come with me? I **must** get to work on time, but once I'm there, we can squeak for a few minutes."

Without waiting for their reply, he scurried away.

The five friends glanced at one another, then hurried after him.

Suddenly, Shinobu slipped through the door of a building. The mouselets were on his heels as he went up some stairs. On the

THIRD floor, he walked through a door.

The THEA SISTERS found themselves inside a tiny café.

"But . . . what are we doing **HERE**?" asked Violet.

"I wouldn't say no to a snack . . ." Pam said.

Colette pointed at Shinobu, who had put on a white shirt and a vest at *LIGHTNING* speed and was standing behind the counter.

"**YOU WORK HERE?**" she asked the rat.

He nodded. "Yes! Would you like to order something?"

"Well, we *FOLLOWED* you to talk . . . remember?" asked Violet.

Shinobu laughed. "Of course! Excuse me — I was running so *late* that I forgot you were behind me!"

Before the Thea Sisters could squeak,

though, a group of customers came in and sat down.

Shinobu winked at the Thea Sisters. "I see I have to get to work. Why don't you sing some songs while you wait for me?"

"What?!" Violet exclaimed. "Why should we sing?"

"Because we have karaoke, and it's fun!" Shinobu said. He gave them microphones and led them to a large screen hanging in the corner of the café. A video of a famouse song was starting, with the lyrics in subtitles on the screen.

"I read that in JAPAN, karaoke is a much-loved tradition," Paulina whispered.

Violet protested, "I don't plan to —"

"La, la, la, laa . . ." Colette had grabbed a microphone, and her squeak burst over the speakers.

Violet sighed. "All right then . . ."

Half an hour and many songs later, the mouselets finally got Shinobu's attention for **five minutes**.

"Do you have a relative named Kyoko Bianchi who also lived in Verona, Italy?"

"I don't think so . . . my dad is Italian,

and so are all my relatives on his side. My mom is Japanese, and she has another last name."

"OH NO!" Pam exclaimed. "Now what?"

"Would you like to sing another song?" Shinobu asked.

"We should get to our hotel. But thank you!" Paulina responded.

When they were back outside, Nicky said, "Squeaking of the hotel . . . how do we get there?"

"Let's take a TAXI!" Colette declared, then hailed one immediately. "To the Capsule Hotel, please!" she said, showing the address to the driver.

"Wait — where's Pam?" asked Nicky.

Their friend arrived out of breath and with her paws full. "I found a kiosk and I bought some basic necessities!"

Sweet crepe with whipped cream

Potato croquettes

Rice dumplings

Rice balls

"I picked up some rice balls, potato croquettes, rice dumplings, and crepes!"

"Great idea!" Nicky smiled. "We were so focused, we forgot to **eat**!"

Shortly after, they arrived at the hotel.

"You are on the fourth floor, capsules seven to eleven," said the receptionist kindly, then pointed. "Lockers for your **baggage** are over there. Have a good stay!"

"Capsules? Lockers? What is she talking about?" Pam asked.

The friends soon discovered why the hotel was called **Capsule**. Instead of rooms, there were "capsules," which were **sleeping cubbies**, similar to beds on a train.

"We haven't EATEN. And our beds are capsules!" Violet complained.

"It's true . . . but we've also visited an

That's why it has that name!

INCREDIBLE city, met some cosplayers, and sung karaoke!" Paulina said, putting a paw around her shoulder.

"I'm sure that tomorrow we'll come up with a good **PLAN** for what to do next," Nicky added. "But for now, let's get into our capsules and try to rest!"

A GARDEN SURPRISE

Their **NIGHT** in the capsules turned out to be much more comfortable than they'd expected. Nicky woke up early the next morning, rested and full of energy — but her friends were still sleeping soundly!

Nicky decided to use her free time to go for a **JOG**. She chose a path around the gardens of the **Imperial Palace** recommended by her guidebook.

After her night in the small capsule, it felt great to be out running in fresh air, next to nature.

At nine, she'd finished her jog and decided

to take a quick walk through the gardens before going back to the hotel. The plants and flowers were in perfect harmony!

Nearby there was a gardener was carefully planting a flower in the soil.

"How beautiful . . ." she whispered.

"Do you like it?" responded the gardener. "It's a *Kyoko Bianchi*, in bloom."

"**A WHAT?!** What did you say it was called?" asked Nicky.

"**Kyoko Bianchi**. Interesting, isn't it? It's named after the mouse who first planted this species, a **passionate** botanist who lived many years ago. Her foundation, the Fairy Garden, still exists today and has wonderful programs to safeguard nature and study plants."

Nicky shook her snout in **SURPRISE**. "Could you . . . could you tell me where this foundation is located?"

The mouse entered the **address** in Nicky's phone. Half an hour later, Nicky joined her friends, who were having breakfast together at a **café** close to the hotel.

"What I would

What is this?

give for a nice croissant . . ." Colette **sighed**.

"Wait, is this chocolate?" asked Paulina, biting into a **PASTRY** with a dark filling. "Oh, what an interesting flavor . . ."

Violet chuckled. "It's a sweet **red bean** paste, made from the adzuki bean. I like it!"

"Mouselets! I discovered something amazing!" Nicky announced.

Four pairs of eyes stared at her, surprised.

"Kyoko Bianchi started a foundation here to protect gardens . . . and I know **where it is**!"

"Fabumouse!" Pam cried. "Let's go — maybe we'll find a new clue there!"

The address the gardener had given them

led them to a large building in the traditional Japanese style, surrounded by a **growing** flower garden. The gate was open, and the Thea Sisters wandered in.

"**How wonderful!**" Colette gushed. "The

gardener told me this place was magical,"
Nicky said. "She was absolutely right!"

A mouse approached them. "Can I help you?" he asked.

"Yes! We're looking for information about KYOKO Bianchi," Violet responded.

"Well, you are in just the right place. Everything here was Ms. Bianchi's idea. My name is Toshio, and I can show you around!"

SEARCHING FOR CLUES

The Fairy Garden Foundation's offices were spread over several floors of the building. Toshio gave the **FIVE FRIENDS** a tour, explaining, "Here, for more than fifty years, scientists and volunteers have worked to defend existing gardens and create new green spaces. Do you see this?" The Thea Sisters saw a large map in the hallway. "These are the gardens that we're currently caring for."

"What a wonderful project!" Nicky said.

"It all started because of Kyoko Bianchi," Toshio replied. "How do you know her?"

Paulina sighed. "It's a very long story . . .

We're connected by one of her Italian friends, from Verona . . ."

"Verona, of course!" he exclaimed. "There's a photo on her desk of her in front of Juliet's balcony — you know, from **Shakespeare's** play?"

"Her desk? You mean that there's still an office for Ms. Kyoko here?!" Pam asked.

Toshio nodded. "It's this way."

He led them to a room full of antique wooden furniture.

"This was **KYOKO'S** office. And here's the picture that I told you about," said Toshio, pointing at a black-and-white photo on her large desk.

Kyoko in Verona

The Thea Sisters recognized the **young mouse** from the photo of her they'd seen in Verona.

"Are there more of Kyoko's photos or papers here?" asked Violet.

Toshio thought for a minute. "I don't think so. The **foundation** wanted to keep the memory of Kyoko alive, but there actually isn't much here that belonged to her. Just this furniture and her **ENCYCLOPEDIA**."

Violet had an idea. "Toshio, would you help us examine the room carefully? We've made a long **journey**, and we can't leave if we're not sure that we've checked everywhere."

Toshio seemed surprised. "Are you looking for something? I can help."

The Thea Sisters started to **LOOK** around the room as they filled him in.

"It seems like this bookshelf is just a huge encyclopedia," Pam observed.

"It's a botanical encyclopedia," Toshio said. "It's a little outdated, but Kyoko asked that we keep it."

"I found something!" Colette exclaimed.

From the bottom of a desk drawer, she pulled out a very thin sheet of rice paper that had traces of logograms* on it.

"It's a short poem," said Toshio, frowning.

He cleared his throat and recited:

> *Inside Jomon Sugi*
> *I left my voice*
> *For whoever wants to hear it.*

"Cheese on a stick!" Pam cried. "What does it mean?"

He explained, "Jomon Sugi is an ancient tree, if that helps."

---

* Logograms are symbols that represent an entire word. Japanese writing uses characters instead of letters, and many characters are logograms.

"Maybe Kyoko left something inside one of the trees in the garden," Colette said.

Toshio looked doubtful. "Jomon Sugi is a specific tree on the island of Yakushima."

"Is that **nearby**?" asked Violet.

"Not at all! I'm sorry, but I think it's just a **POEM** . . ." responded Toshio.

"Toshio, you said that this botanical encyclopedia was hers, right?" Nicky asked. "Maybe **KYOKO** wrote a message in the entry for this tree!"

"**Great idea**, Nicky! Toshio, would you be able to find the right volume?" asked Paulina.

"Here it is," the ratlet said, then set the large book on the desk. "Strange — it's not very heavy."

When Colette opened the book, everyone **squeaked** in amazement.

A rectangular space was cut out of the pages themselves, and a large black videotape was inside!

LET'S GO!

Nicky took out the cassette and lifted it up. **"What is this?"**

"It's a VHS videotape," Paulina responded.

"I bet Kyoko recorded a video on it many years ago . . ." Toshio said.

"Fabumouse!" Colette said cheerfully. "That means we can watch it and hear her message!"

"That would be great . . ." Paulina sighed. "But this technology is very old. We'd have to find a VHS player, or someone who could convert it into a digital version."

"Ren!" exclaimed Toshio.

"What?!" the mouselets squeaked.

"Ren is a good friend who is an expert in

old **technologies**, programs, or recording devices that have been replaced by newer versions, so no one uses them anymore. I'm sure he could help us."

"Then let's go find him!" Nicky said.

"There's one a **small problem**," Toshio said. "Ren doesn't live in Tokyo — he lives in Kyoto, a city about **three hundred miles** from here."

"Well, isn't Japan famouse for its **SUPER-FAST** trains?" Colette asked with a big smile.

I don't understand...

And so, a few hours later, the Thea Sisters were at the **TRAIN** station, about to board the bullet train to Kyoto. This high-speed train would bring them to their destination in just over two hours!

"Where is Toshio? He said he'd meet us here," Paulina muttered, looking around.

"There he is!" said Pam, pointing at a mouse tottering under a high stack of packages.

The Thea Sisters hurried to lighten his load. The packages were trays with lots of small COMPARTMENTS that were filled with colorful foods.

"I decided to buy lunch," Toshio explained. "But we need to **BOARD** the train: In exactly ten seconds, it will leave the station!"

On the train, Pam took a closer look at the trays.

"They're **bento boxes**, typical Japanese portable lunch boxes!" Toshio said.

Nicky smiled. "Not only

are you taking us to see your friend, you also brought local specialties for us to eat! Thank you so much!"

"You're welcome!" Toshio said. "I hope Ren can help us!"

A LEAP INTO THE PAST

The Thea Sisters noticed immediately that Kyoto was very different from the bustling city of Tokyo. Toshio took them to Ren's house, which was in a very traditional neighborhood. As the mouselets walked through the stone streets scattered with little shops and low **WOODEN** buildings, they felt as if they'd fallen into another world.

"This is the **Higashiyama** district, which has kept the traditional feel of historic Kyoto," explained Toshio.

"It's very beautiful," Colette said.

"You're going to love Ren's house!" Toshio replied.

Ren's house was an old wooden building that was perfectly preserved. As soon as they entered, Toshio motioned for them to take off their shoes and put on the **slippers** that were there for guests. The floor was covered with woven straw mats.

"These are tatami mats," Toshio said. "And . . . here is Ren!"

He wore a dark jacket over a long, elegant traditional Japanese dress, and a pair of thong sandals.

He bowed to them, then said, "I'm Ren. Paulina, Pam, Nicky, Colette, Violet: Welcome."

"It's a pleasure to meet you!" responded the Thea Sisters.

Ren immediately burst out laughing, "What's wrong, you didn't expect a technology expert to be so fond of tradition? Toshio, didn't you prepare them?"

Toshio chuckled and turned to the five friends. "As you can see, Ren has great passion for history . . ."

"Like this!" Colette exclaimed, holding out the **videotape**.

Ren smiled, then took the videotape. "Please take a seat at the tea table," he said. *"I'll take care of this!"*

The Thea Sisters and Toshio sat down on the soft cushions that were around the table. Meanwhile, Ren went over to a small cabinet nearby and **fiddled around** for a few seconds. Then he said, "I'm going to prepare some tea. Happy viewing!"

The Thea Sisters realized the cabinet held an old television connected to an old video recorder that still **worked**.

After a few seconds, the screen flickered and the recording appeared. It showed a room containing a beautiful plant with **PINK FLOWERS** and a simple wooden chair.

"How do you . . . It must have started!" a female squeak said from out of the frame.

A second later, a slender figure appeared in the scene and sat down on the chair.

"**IT'S HER! IT'S KYOKO!**" Colette exclaimed. The snout on-screen was much older, but it was clearly the same mouse who'd been in the photo with Linda.

THE TRUE TREASURE

Kyoko settled into her chair and cleared her throat. "Dear viewer, I don't know who you are, but if you were able to find this tape, you must be clever. And if you paid attention to the poem I left behind, you also must have a sensitive **heart**."

Nicky smiled to herself. It felt like those words were just for her! Then she looked **AROUND** and realized that, as always, it had been a team effort. A team of the best friends she could wish for!

Kyoko continued. "I once had a great friend. She was a special mouse, full of life and joy. She helped me discover the **Mysteries** of Verona many years ago."

Pam gasped. "She's talking about Linda!"

The others nodded while the video continued. "At the time, I didn't **imagine** that meeting my friend Linda would change my life, leading me to such a **BIG** decision. I wasn't even twenty years old, and I had to choose whether to become the guardian of one of the most precious **treasures** on Earth . . ."

Ren returned with a **steaming** teapot.

"Yes, you heard that correctly," Kyoko said on-screen. "I was a young Japanese mouse visiting distant relatives in Italy, and I ended up in a game much larger than myself."

Her snout darkened. "It was dangerous. But I accepted my destiny, and I kept the treasure that Linda had given me. And if you're wondering what that treasure is . . ."

Kyoko brought her paw to the center of the video screen. She wore a beautiful **RING** with an intense red stone, which sparkled like a burning flame. "This is the Ring of True Love, given by Romeo to Juliet as a token of his feelings."

"**Ohhh!**" Pam exclaimed, and Colette sighed. No one could **LOOK AWAY** from the screen.

Ren said calmly, pouring tea, "Impossible. Juliet didn't really exist — Shakespeare invented her."

Almost as if she had heard him, **KYOKO** burst into a clear laugh on-screen. "Of course, that's just a legend. But the **truth** is not so different. The stone is ancient, and the ring was a gift from a suitor to a young Cappelletti. That's where Juliet's last name, Capulet, comes from. The young mice were from **feuding** families, just as they are in the play . . . but their families put aside their rivalry when they realized how true the love was. It was a happy ending that Juliet did not have, and it makes this ring a symbol of **love** winning."

"That makes more sense," Ren said, nodding.

Kyoko rested her paw on her lap and stared at the ring's jewel.

"Unfortunately, Aurora could never come back for the ring, but I've guarded it my whole life as if it were the most precious treasure. And now it's time to **pass it on** to someone trustworthy . . ."

The Thea Sisters were startled: Would she tell them where the treasure was?

Kyoko looked directly into the camera and said, "Love is the purest emotion that we can feel, and I'm leaving this ring to a mouse who shows love *every day, in every way, toward everything that grows from the earth*."

The image blurred, and then the screen went black.

"Nooo!" Nicky cried. "What happened? Did the video **BREAK**?"

THE STORY OF THE RING OF TRUE LOVE

Two young mice loved each other but belonged to rival families that didn't approve of their relationship.

The ratlet gave the mouselet a ring set with a perfect ruby as a sign of his love.

Their families saw their feelings were true and allowed them to get married.

Ren shook his snout. "No, that's just the end of it."

"B-but — what — ?" Colette stuttered. "She didn't tell us who she gave the ring to!"

"Maybe she didn't want to give too much away," Toshio guessed. "After all, it's a very precious treasure that she's kept a **SECRET** her entire life. It makes sense that she didn't say everything in one recording!"

"True — if the tape ended up in the wrong paws, it would've been a **disaster**," Violet said. "So it's good that Kyoko was cautious . . . but now we're back to square one!"

BEFORE
LEAVING ° ° °

The mice finished sipping their tea in silence.

"What time is it?" Violet asked, yawning.

"It's evening," Paulina said. "We didn't realize how quickly time PASSED . . ."

"Should we take a night train back to Tokyo?" Colette suggested.

"I would be happy to host you here in Kyoto tonight!" Ren said.

As he headed toward the kitchen, Nicky tried to protest. "But . . . we don't want to **bother** you, and you've already helped us with the video . . ."

"Nonsense," Ren replied, shaking his head. "You must stay."

Ren prepared a **dinner** of rice and vegetables, which everyone ate without squeaking much. The eventful day had left the THEA SISTERS tired and quiet.

Sigh . . .

"What a pity to not be able to solve this mystery," Paulina said **sadly**.

"But seeing Kyoko was **exciting** . . . and something tells me that this isn't over yet," Colette replied.

"Toshio, could you give me a paw preparing the futons?" Ren called from the next room.

The Thea Sisters soon **settled** onto the five futons. The beds were different from their typical idea of a futon, and they may have looked simple, but they were

comfortable! In a few minutes, the friends were all asleep.

"**Good morning, mouselets!**" Ren's squeak woke them the next day.

"Is it already time to **leave**?" Colette asked.

"No, your train leaves in a few hours. But

How comfortable!

Good night, girls!

I thought you might like to see a bit of the city while you're here . . ."

"Fabumouse!" Nicky said. "I'd love to be in the OPEN AIR for a while before I'm closed up in a train!"

"Five more minutes, please . . ." Violet murmured from under her pillow.

Half an hour later, the mouselets were dressed and ready to go out.

"Where are we headed?" Paulina asked.

"It's a surprise," Ren said, smiling.

After a brief bus ride, the group found itself in front of a huge ancient wooden entry gate, ornately decorated in gold.

"Welcome to Nijo Castle!" Ren said. "It was constructed in the early seventeenth century and later became an imperial home. Come on, let's go in — this section is the **Ninomaru Palace!**"

The mice admired the architecture of the castle and its wonderful atmosphere. In one hall, they heard a strange chirping noise coming from the floor as they walked.

"The nails and clamps under the floorboards make this noise, but it's said to sound like birdsong," Toshio said.

"In fact, this is called the nightingale corridor," Ren said. "But time is running out — let's visit the garden."

Outside the palace, the Thea Sisters gazed in awe at a magnificent Japanese garden with a large pond, pine trees, and elegant ornamental stones. It looked lush and harmonious.

Nicky took a deep breath. "What a splendid experience! Thank you, Ren!"

"Thanks to you for honoring me with your visit," Ren responded. "But now I think

we'd better **GET GOING**."

"Where's Violet?" Paulina asked, a little worried.

"She was here a minute ago," Colette said. "There she is."

Their friend was bent over a small plant, so focused that she didn't realize the others were approaching.

"**Love toward everything that grows from the earth . . .**" they heard her say.

"Vi, is everything okay?" Pam asked.

Violet smiled. "It's more than okay. I think I know who has Juliet's ring!"

THE FINAL PIECE

BZZZ . . . BZZZZZZ . . . BZZZ . . . BZZZZZZZ . . .

Cassidy was busy soldering, but she stopped her work, pushed up her protective **goggles**, and reached for her wrist communicator to answer the incoming call.

"So, how far are you?" Luke von Klawitz squeaked from the tiny **SCREEN**.

"Good morning, sir . . ." Cassidy said.

"Have you **finished**?" he asked.

"I'm at a good point," she replied. "I've almost

finished putting the engine into the frame. The **MOTHERBOARD*** that you sent me from Alaska is perfect. Then I'll just have to —"

"Forget the technical details!" Luke interrupted. "I just want to know when it will be ready."

"Tonight, just as I planned, sir," his assistant said proudly. "It hasn't been easy, but I'm happy with the wor —"

The screen went black. Luke had hung up.

Cassidy sighed, put her googles back on, and went back to work.

"Luckily, I have master's degrees in **engineering**, **chemistry**, and computer ſcience," she muttered as she

---

* A motherboard is the central part of a computer that holds essential components and allows communication between them.

adjusted various components on the device she was assembling.

Just then someone knocked on her hotel room door, making her JUMP.

"Who is it?"

"It's me. I have what you need," said a squeak on the other side of the door.

Here it is!

Great!

Cassidy opened the door for Omar, who held a PACKAGE.

"Here's the camera."

"It took you long enough," Cassidy said sourly.

"I got it from a safe-deposit box, and there was a long process," Omar said. "Here in **JAPAN**, everyone is always trying to be helpful and too polite, which wastes a lot of time . . ."

"I know, it's a **pain**," Cassidy said coldly. Then she opened the package. "Perfect!" she squeaked. "It's the last piece to install. Then the drone* will be ready, and we'll discover where Juliet's treasure is hidden!"

* A drone is an aircraft that is flown from far away (via a computer) without a pilot on board.

A KIND HEART

Meanwhile, the THEA SISTERS and Toshio had taken the train back to Tokyo. Ren had joined them as well. He felt invested in Kyoko's story, and wanted to help discover what had happened to her precious treasure!

The friends arrived back at the Fairy Garden Foundation.

"**Here we are!**" Nicky announced.

"So, this is the famous foundation that you work for, Toshio," Ren said, turning to his friend.

"Yes — and it only took five visitors from

Whale Island to get you to come SEE it!" Toshio teased him.

"What it really took was a great mystery," said Ren with a smile.

Violet was scanning the gardens.

"Do you see him?" Paulina asked.

"No . . ."

"I do!" Colette cried, pointing to the far corner of the grounds. "He's down there!"

The mice RAN over to a figure bent over a flower bed.

"Mr. Murakami?" Toshio said.

"Good morning, Toshio," Mr. Murakami said with a calm smile. "Did you bring some new friends for a visit?"

Toshio nodded and introduced them. "These are the Thea Sisters, and my childhood friend Ren."

Then Toshio turned to his friends. "This is Mr. Murakami, the foundation's **gardener** for . . ."

"Fifty-nine years," he said. "I was only a mouseling when I **began** to work here, thanks to the generosity of Ms. Bianchi."

"So you knew **KYOKO**!" Colette said, excited.

"Ah, you know her name," the old mouse said **kindly**. "Maybe because of the plant dedicated to her?"

Toshio said, "It's a bit **MORE** than that. Could we go to the greenhouse and squeak a bit?"

In the greenhouse, the young mice told **Mr. Murakami** the whole story.

"And so, when I heard that Kyoko left the **treasure** to someone who showed love every day toward everything that grows from the earth, I thought that it might be a **gardener**," Violet explained.

"And I told them that **KYOKO'S** personal gardener was still here . . . which is you!" Toshio concluded.

Mr. Murakami went silent for a long moment.

Then he said, "That's a fascinating story

and I am honored. But what makes you think that Kyoko would leave me something so precious?"

"Well, we think she would have chosen someone who was kind, HONEST, and attentive," began Nicky.

"Someone who could take care of delicate things, like an antique treasure," Colette continued.

At that moment, a bird came through the door of the greenhouse in a flurry of wings. It was disoriented and ran into a glass wall.

Worried, Nicky took the bird delicately in her paws, being careful to not crush it or startle it. Then she took it outside and let it fly away.

"Wow, that was awesome," Pam said, cheering. "Great job, sister!"

Mr. Murakami had been **WATCHING**, and a smile appeared on his snout.

"I see in you the qualities you mentioned before. Kyoko, who remained a dear friend, always said: **'True strength lies in a kind heart.'**"

IN THE HEART OF THE PARK

Violet exclaimed, "I knew it! She did leave Juliet's ring with you!"

Mr. Murakami nodded. "I didn't think anyone would come looking for it. Many years have passed since Kyoko asked me to hide it and protect it at any cost. That's why I couldn't trust you right away."

Colette interjected, "Could we ask . . . *where is the treasure now*?"

The old mouse got up and said, "We must take a trip."

You're the guardian!

"That's nothing **NEW** for us!" Pam quipped.

Paulina said, "A trip where, Mr. Murakami?"

Kyoko Bianchi and
Mr. Murakami

"To my birth city," he said with a smile.

"Nara?!" Toshio exclaimed.

The gardener nodded. "That is where we'll find what you are looking for."

A little more than four **HOURS** later, the Thea Sisters, Ren, Toshio, and Mr. Murakami got off the train in Nara. As the gardener led them toward his **hiding place** for the treasure, they were soon surrounded by green.

"We are in Nara Park, one of the oldest parks in **JAPAN**. Here, more than a thousand specimens of our national treasure live —"

"Hey, guys, there are a bunch of stalls selling crackers!" Pam interrupted. "I just bought a pack. Do you want one?"

Ren, Toshio, and Mr. Murakami exchanged an AMUSED look.

"Pam, those crackers aren't for us," Ren began to explain. "LOOK behind you, and you'll see . . ."

Pam turned — and found herself a few inches from the nose of a large deer with elegant antlers. "Great Gorgonzola! Where did you come from?"

In response, the deer NUDGED her with his nose.

"I think that he wants a snack!" Nicky said, laughing.

Another deer approached Pam, and

then another
and another! Soon
she was surrounded.

Pam distributed the crackers
to her new four-legged friends.

"What a charming place,"

Ha, ha, ha!

Um . . . how
can I help you?

Colette said, petting a fawn that had come up to her.

"I'm happy **you like it**," Mr. Murakami replied. "But now, come with me."

The friends followed him deeper into the marvemouse park, admiring the BEAUTY of the plants and deer on the way.

Finally, Mr. Murakami stopped in a *WILDER* and more solitary corner of the park. He approached a large tree and began to count his pawsteps. When he got to sixteen, he stopped.

"This is it . . . but . . ."

The friends saw the peaceful calm fade from **Mr. Murakami's** snout for the first time. It was replaced with dismay.

"Is everything okay?" asked Nicky. As she approached, she understood what had shocked him: Next to a large boulder, the earth was loose where someone had dug a deep **Hole**.

"The treasure . . . the treasure was here!" muttered Mr. Murakami.

"What happened to it?" Nicky cried.

"Are . . . are you sure this was the spot?" Paulina asked.

"Yes, it was here: sixteen steps north of the camphor tree . . ."

"Someone found it before us," Ren concluded, seeing the hole.

"But who could it have been? And how

did they know it was here?" asked Toshio.

Mr. Murakami shook his snout. "I don't know. It was in a box inside a **SAFE**, buried deep."

"It had to have been **LUKE VON KLAWITZ**!" Colette said. "He beat us to it."

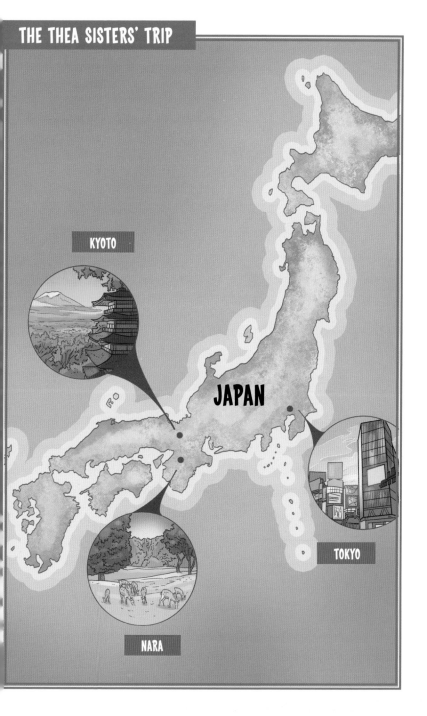

THE THEA SISTERS' TRIP

KYOTO

JAPAN

TOKYO

NARA

NEW DISCOVERIES

The Thea Sisters started to investigate. They asked **Mr. Murakami**, "When is the last time you were here?"

"Just two days ago . . ."

"And was everything okay with the treasure?" asked Paulina.

"Yes, the **SAFE** was in place."

"Did you notice anything unusual?"

"No . . ."

"Apart from you," asked Violet, "did anyone else know of this **hiding spot**?"

"No! Kyoko and I came up with how and where to hide the treasure. I've never revealed it to anyone before you! I guarded that treasure my whole life, and now . . ."

"Try not to worry — we'll find it!" Colette said to **calm** him.

"Maybe we should sit down and have some tea," said Toshio.

"In the **PARK**, there's a *chaya*: a teahouse," Ren said. "Why don't you go there? I'll stay here and **LOOK AROUND** . . . There could be a useful clue."

"I'll stay with you," said Nicky.

The other mice took the gardener to the **teahouse**.

"I'll look over here, and you look over there, okay?" Nicky said to Ren. He nodded, and they

I failed . . .

We'll find it!

immediately began to search.

Nicky started poking around without knowing what she was **LOOKING** for. She came across a deer grazing in front of a bush.

"Are you here to help me?" she asked, smiling.

The deer stared at her for a moment with sweet, dark **EYES**, then scampered away.

Something behind the bush caught Nicky's

attention. "**What's that?**" she asked herself. It was metal. She went up to it, and immediately called out, "Ren, come here, please . . ."

He joined her, asking, "Did something happen?" Then he saw the object and said, "Why is there a **drone** here?"

"A drone? You mean one of those flying robot things that take pictures?" asked Nicky.

A drone?!

"That's an interesting definition, but yes," Ren said, kneeling to LOOK at it more closely. "It's broken, but it's a very advanced and expensive model."

"Of course! Luke von Klawitz would never use something cheap!" Nicky said bitterly.

"Who?" asked Ren. He didn't know the whole story.

"Do you see this TAG?" Nicky said, pointing to a small metal plate on the corner of the drone. "These are Luke von Klawitz's initials and his company logo. He's the selfish mouse who's trying to get his paws on all the treasures collected by Aurora Beatrix Lane."

"Looks like he managed to track down Juliet's ring."

"It seems so. Let's go tell the others, and

bring the drone!" Nicky said.

Meanwhile, the other Thea Sisters were sipping green tea with Toshio and Mr. Murakami.

"To open the safe, you had to know a certain word, which Kyoko had given me," the gardener was explaining. Then he smiled and continued. "A word that had always made me laugh . . . **MONKEY!**"

"Of course!" exclaimed Colette. "It was a nickname that Aurora had at the university. Remember? We read it in her **DIARY** . . ."

"Look!" Pam interrupted her, **POINTING** at Nicky and Ren walking around the corner. "What are they carrying?"

Paulina stood up. "A **drone**!"

"We found it near the treasure's hiding place," Nicky explained. "And it has the Klawitz logo . . ."

"What did they need a drone for?" asked Colette.

Ren thought for a minute. "Maybe to investigate the area?"

"Or maybe to fOLLOW the movements of Mr. Murakami when he last came to check on the treasure," Violet said.

"Crusty cheddar! They managed to find it and take it before us," Nicky said sadly.

A SIX-LETTER PUZZLE

On the other side of the **world**, Luke von Klawitz waited for his assistants to arrive. He paced nervously in his headquarters in the depths of **ALASKA**.

"How long does it take? Those incompetent fools!" he muttered.

Then he went back to the **control room** and grabbed the notebook that belonged to his grandfather Jan von Klawitz.

"This time, I did it. I was able to complete your mission . . ." he whispered, carefully turning the **PAGES** that had yellowed over time.

Luke had just finished reading the page when the room's **electronic** door

I have not yet been able to solve the riddle of the Treasure of True Love. The thought of that little mouselet taking it from under my snout fills me with anger. "Monkey," as everyone called her when she was still my student — because of her curiosity and kindness.

But monkeys are also sneaky and cunning. She managed to take this treasure and hide it who knows where! But one day, I'm sure, not long from now, I'll recover all seven treasures of the world — and no silly little monkey will stop me!

opened and Cassidy and Omar appeared.

Omar held a small metal safe with both paws.

"Good morning, sir," Cassidy said. "As you requested, we brought you —"

"Let me see it!" Luke boomed, not listening.

Here is the safe . . .

Omar placed the safe on the metal floor and Luke EXAMINED it.

"The combination to open it must not be a numerical code," Omar explained. "Instead of numbers on the dial, there are letters."

"We need a KEY WORD," Cassidy concluded.

"Well, aren't you clever," Luke said sarcastically. Then he stared in silence at the dial.

"We checked: It's **SIX** letters," Omar said.

"A word with six letters, so . . ." Luke mused. Then he suddenly exclaimed, "Of course!"

He reached toward the dial and spelled: A-U-R-O-R-A.

"You're a genius!" Cassidy cried.

But the safe remained closed.

"**T-R-E-A-S-U-R-E** . . . No, that's too many letters," Luke muttered.

Then he brightened with an idea. He took his grandfather's notebook and began to laugh.

"But of course! Of course!"

Cassidy and Omar exchanged a puzzled look.

Luke von Klawitz turned the dial to spell the word MONKEY.

The safe opened with a *CLACK!*

Luke delicately raised the LID.

"It's the treasure!" Cassidy squeaked, gripped with excitement.

For a moment, the whole room seemed illuminated by the fiery glow of the large,

The treasure!

Ohh!

pure ruby set in the legendary *Ring of True Love*.

"Oh . . ." Omar said, bewitched.

Luke von Klawitz stared at it greedily.

"Finally, you're mine . . . My display case has been empty for far too long!"

iLLUMiNATiNG PHOTOS

The Thea Sisters weren't going to give up. Luke von Klawitz had **beaten** them to the treasure this time, but not all was lost. They could still track down the ring, get it back, and keep it **SAFE**, as Aurora would have wanted.

See you soon!

Mr. Murakami had decided to stay in Nara with family to rest and recover from the awful surprise. The mouselets and Toshio had accepted Ren's invitation to return to his house in Kyoto (which was closer to Nara), to study the drone together and see if it contained any other clues.

"Paulina, can you give me a paw?" Ren asked as they entered the house. "I want to get the motherboard out of the drone and see if we can get any images or **other data** from it."

"Sounds good!" Paulina said.

Ren showed her the corner where he kept his **computer**, and the two got to work. The others started to go through everything they knew about what had happened.

After a moment, Pam's stomach grumbled. "Is anyone else hungry?" she asked. "I can't think with an **EMPTY** belly!"

Ren heard her and said, "Feel free to fix yourself something if you want!"

Pam didn't make him say it twice! In no time, she was peeling, slicing, and frying. The house filled with the **smell** of delicious food.

"What did you make?" asked Colette.

"I followed the recipe for ramen with vegetables," Pam said nervously. "It's a Japanese noodle soup. I hope I made it correctly!"

"**It smells delicious!**" Toshio said. "I didn't know you were a cook!"

"Our Pam is an expert on everything from engines to stoves!" said Nicky. "Shall we head to the table?"

"Great idea!" Colette said. "Paulina! Ren! Join us!"

"Just a second!" Paulina said. She and Ren soon joined their friends at the table, smiling.

Ramen with vegetables

"Would you like some ramen?" Pam offered.

Paulina nodded. "Yes, please — but first,

you need to see what we found!" She placed her **TABLET** on the table. "I downloaded the photos that were saved in the memory of the drone," she explained.

"And even though it was damaged, we still managed to **RECOVER** a lot of interesting images," Ren added. "These are the views of Nara Park."

"There's Mr. Murakami!" Nicky said. "They were **spying** on him like we thought!"

NARA PARK

Paulina confirmed, "This must be how they found the treasure's hiding place."

"But that's not all," Ren said. "Look, these are the first images taken by the drone . . ."

The next photos showed a beautiful mountain landscape.

"Mountains . . . moose . . . bears . . . This doesn't seem like JAPAN!" commented Nicky.

"It's not," Ren confirmed. "They're in ALASKA!"

ALASKA

"Cheese and crackers!" Pam said. "What does Alaska have to do with this?"

"Ren and I think the photos were taken before the drone was sent out on its mission," Paulina said.

"That means they could have been taken near . . . Luke von Klawitz's **headquarters**!" yelled Violet, following her intuition.

"Exactly! Which gives us a new lead in our mission," Paulina said.

Pam smiled. "**We're going to Alaska!**"

LEAVING AGAIN

It was time to say good-bye to their Japanese friends and depart on a new leg of their journey.

"I printed out a little guide to Alaska. I hope it's useful," Ren said, pawing a small BOOKLET to Colette.

"Thank you! That is so kind," Colette said. "We don't know what awaits us up there . . ."

"And we must be very careful," Violet added. "Klawitz will do anything to protect his wealth, and his assistants are just as bad."

Ren gave Paulina a flash drive.* "Here are

* A flash drive is a small electronic data-storing device often used to transport files. It can be plugged in to any device with a USB port.

some programs I **wrote** that could help."

"Thank you," Paulina said softly. "It was really **wonderful** to meet you. And you've helped us so much!"

"It was great to meet you, too. You have to let us know what happens!"

"Of course, we'll **stay in touch** — and let us know when you come visit Whale Island!"

Toshio appeared at the front door. "We have to go. The **TRAIN** won't wait for us!"

"Thanks again, Ren!" the mouselets said together, then left Kyoto.

Toshio took them to the Tokyo airport in a **CAR**.

"Say good-bye to Mr. Murakami for us," Paulina said.

"Of course!" Toshio replied.

"We hope so . . ." Pam said as they headed

into the **AIRPORT**. "Good-bye, Toshio, and thank you for everything!"

After they dropped their **baggage** off at check-in, Nicky commented,

"Coco, I'm a little jealous of your huge backpack. I've been wearing the same clothes for three days!"

Colette smiled. "I have two words for you: duty-free."

"What do you mean?" Pam asked.

"We still have forty-five minutes before our departure, and there are a bunch of fabumouse airport stores just waiting for us!"

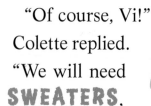

"Is now really the time to go shopping?" Violet asked, unsure.

Cozy socks

"Of course, Vi!" Colette replied. "We will need **SWEATERS**, cozy **SOCKS**, and warm **hats**!"

Warm hat

Heavy sweater

"Sweaters, socks, and hats?" repeated Violet.

"For **ALASKA**! It's a cold place," Colette said with a smile.

"Sisters, something tells me that we cannot escape at least half an hour of *shopping* with Coco . . ." Nicky said.

"Great Gouda! This store is the perfect place to begin!" Colette shrieked, rushing toward a shopwindow.

HIGH-ALTITUDE READING

While they were boarding the airplane, the Thea Sisters realized they were not sitting together.

Only Colette and Nicky happened to be next to each other, near a **WINDOW** in the middle of the plane. Paulina was in the row in front of them, Violet was way at the back, and Pam was over in the middle aisle.

"I guess we'll have to FLY separately," Nicky said.

The mouse sitting next to her heard and asked, "Would you like me to **trade** seats with your friend?"

"That would be so kind!" Colette smiled.

Pam was happy to sit by her friends.

Paulina LEANED back toward the trio. "We can still talk!"

"Buckle your seat belts, please!" the flight attendant said as she passed by.

"What about Vi? Can she move over, too?" Colette asked.

Paulina PEERED back, then sat down and fastened her seat belt.

"Don't worry . . . Vi is already snoring!" She laughed.

"She'll miss the reading we had planned to do on this flight . . ." Nicky said, pulling out one of Aurora's letters.

"How many are left to read?" asked Paulina.

"Two!" Colette said. "And I don't know about you, but I can't wait to find out what else Aurora told her sister . . ."

"Read it!" the others squeaked.

May 12

Dear Amaryllis,

I'm very sorry that, because of my job, you are taking on a responsibility that is perhaps too great, and that puts you at risk.

It's all because of the greed of my former professor, a mouse who is incapable of recognizing that beauty should be shared. My dear sister, I have thought about it for a long time, and I have come to the conclusion that the best solution is to take the Treasure of True Love out of Verona, where it is not safe . . . and where it puts you at risk.

I am sending you a copy of one of the photos I hold the most dear, in memory of the love that binds us. I hope it will help you make the best decision . . .

Yours,
Aurora

"Poor Aurora! She was so worried about her sister even though she herself was in danger on her **MISSION** to recover the seven treasures," Nicky said. "She always put her family ahead of herself."

"She was truly an exceptional rodent!" Colette said.

"Good thing she had her **sisters** to count on!" Paulina exclaimed, startling the mouse who was sitting next to her. "They were all pretty exceptional."

Nicky nodded. "It's true. Any mouse who has friends and sisters beside her is very lucky. And we know that Linda did exactly as Aurora suggested: She made the best decision to keep the treasure safe."

"Let's read the last letter," Colette suggested. "Maybe we'll discover something new . . ."

May 28

Dear Amaryllis,

You wrote me that you are making a decision about the treasure. I agree that the mouse you're planning to entrust it to is worthy of that trust, and I will wait for more news. But you must be careful, even when you write to me, to not mention names or places. We need to watch out, because my former professor is more alert than ever.

It seems that he's building an underground shelter for his riches, designed as a kind of maze to test anyone who manages to enter it . . .

Professor Jan is clever, and he's always loved riddles, puzzles, and mysteries. I wouldn't wish for any mouse to find themselves in that maze!

Now I must say good-bye, my dear. Sending a big hug.

Yours,
Aurora

Colette said, "What a ridiculous mouse Klawitz was — even his secret shelter was built like a MAZE!"

"And his grandson doesn't seem to be any less ridiculous . . . He's given us a lot of **trouble**," Pam said.

Who knows what awaits us . . .

"Let's at least hope he doesn't have the same taste for puzzles and the headquarters we're going to isn't full of TRAPS!" Paulina added.

ON THE MARCH!

Soon, the Thea Sisters got out of the airport in Anchorage, Alaska. They hurried to rent an SUV so they could drive north. They wanted to get to the spot that Ren and Paulina had located thanks to the drone's photographs as quickly as they could.

"Come on, sisters! **we're on the march!**" Pam squeaked as she got behind the wheel.

Paulina typed the location into the MousePhone **GPS** and took the seat next to her so that she could navigate.

Violet read some information about **ALASKA** from the guide Ren printed for them.

ALASKA

Alaska is part of the United States, but it does not touch any other US states. To the east, it borders **Canada**, and to the west, the **Bering Strait** separates it from Siberia, Russia. To its north is the **Arctic Ocean** and to the south, the **Pacific Ocean**.

The biggest city in Alaska is Anchorage. The climate is cold (though some areas can get warm in the summer). The lowest temperature recorded is -80° Fahrenheit!

Its territory contains many species of birds, such as albatross and eagles, as well as many mammals, such as **black bears** and **grizzly bears**, **wolves, moose, caribou, lynx, coyotes, foxes, beavers**, and a species of wild sheep with big horns called **Dall sheep**.

Alaskan forests are mainly **pine trees,** along with birch and aspen. The state is also full of **mosses, lichen, fungi,** and many **flowering plants.** Many areas sit on **permafrost,** which is ground that remains permanently frozen.

The mouselets felt nervous. Soon they would find themselves snout-to-snout with their rival, Luke von Klawitz. They didn't know exactly what awaited them, but if Luke followed in the footsteps of his grandfather Jan — whom Aurora described as greedy and dishonest — surely it was nothing good.

"Hey, is that a moose?" Colette asked, pointing at a **LARGE** animal plodding along calmly not far from the road.

"Where? Yes, it is! How fabumouse!" Nicky exclaimed, leaning toward the window.

"Hey, watch out! You're squishing me!" Violet complained.

"I'm sorry, Vi . . . but you know how much I **love** nature!" Nicky said.

"I know, let's pull over so we can switch

seats," Violet responded.

"Mouselets, isn't this amazing?" asked Pam, who was enjoying the drive.

"IT'S INCREDIBLE," Nicky agreed.

"Klawitz couldn't have picked a more beautiful place for his base," Colette said, **admiring** the dense grassy fields, trees, and mountains that rose to the <u>horizon</u>.

Their drive continued peacefully, and the

friends managed to keep their spirits high by joking and **laughing**.

Squeak!

Suddenly, Paulina said, "Pam, **PARK** the car behind those large trees. We should go the rest of the way by paw."

"You got it!" She stopped the SUV near a **fir tree**, and the Thea Sisters got out.

Paulina explained, "According to the **MAP** in the guide that Ren printed for us, the base shouldn't be more than a ten-minute walk . . ."

"There won't be any

FEROCIOUS animals, right?" Colette asked, a little timidly.

Violet responded, "Coco, I think the mouse we'll encounter at the base is the most FEROCIOUS thing we'll meet . . ."

After they walked a bit, Paulina stopped. "According to the directions, Klawitz's base is . . . here!"

The friends LOOKED at one another uncertainly.

"Are you sure? I only see grass, trees, and stones . . ." Pam said.

"Nothing that looks like the kind of headquarters we're looking for," Violet added.

Paulina LOOKED at the map and then at her phone. "You're right, but still: This is the spot that was photographed by the drone!"

"Maybe Klawitz and his accomplices sent it here on a scouting trip? Or it could've been here to look for who knows what other treasure!" Colette sighed. "What if we're completely on the WRONG track?!"

She slumped down onto the grass unhappily. And at that moment, the earth began to vibrate.

UNEXPECTED LANDING

"D-did you feel that, too?" Colette barely had time to ask before the earth underneath them suddenly gave way!

"AAAAAAAAAAAAHHHH!" the Thea Sisters screamed, slipping downward *FASTER* than the mouse ran up the clock.

Suddenly, they landed on something soft.

THUMP!

AAAAAAHHH!

It was dimly lit and **smelled** terrible.

"Sweet stinky cheese! Are you okay, sisters?" Pam asked.

"Ow! You elbowed me!" Colette said — she'd landed partly underneath Pam.

"I'm all in one piece," Nicky said from not far away. Violet confirmed, "Me too!"

"We're missing Paulina. **PAULINA?!**" Colette yelled into the darkness.

"Be quiet! They'll hear us!" Paulina responded quietly from another corner of that **D A R K** room.

"Sorry!" whispered Colette. "I was worried. But who is 'they'?"

"Luke von Klawitz," Paulina said. "I think we're in his **SECRET HEADQUARTERS!**"

"And I think I have a banana peel on my shoulder," Nicky said.

"I think we're in trash bins," Violet said.

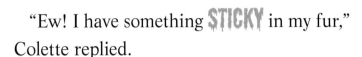

"Ew! I have something STICKY in my fur," Colette replied.

"Thanks to the trash, we landed on something soft," Violet said. "Plus, if there are security cameras around, they probably don't cover the garbage dump . . . so they might not know we're here!"

Nicky climbed out of the dumpster that she'd landed in and LOOKED around. "Hey,

this looks like the wing of an old **plane**!" she said.

Pam approached another METAL object. "This seems like the propeller blades of a helicopter!"

"This place is full of pieces of old aircraft," Violet added, joining the others.

What a strange place!

Colette sighed. "It can't be said that it was a **grand** entrance . . ."

"You're right, Coco — it wasn't the one that we'd imagined. But the important thing is that we weren't **discovered**!" Nicky said.

"I still don't understand how we landed down here on all this trash!" Pam said.

Paulina explained, "We went through that **tube** over the bins, see? I think that it's a vacuum elevator, used to get objects in and out. We probably **activated it** from above automatically by pressing some point on the ground, and the tube sucked us down here."

"You said ELEVATOR, right? So it also leads up and we can get out?" asked Nicky, sounding panicked. "I really don't like this closed-in room. It feels like a bunker . . ."

"Stay calm!" exclaimed Colette. "The trash must be brought into here from somewhere else, right? So there must be a **CONNECTION** with the rest of the building. Which means an exit for us!"

"Or better yet, an entrance . . . to **KLAWITZ'S** base," Violet said.

The friends began to explore the room, pressing on walls.

After a few minutes, Paulina squeaked, "I found it! This way, sisters — there's a **HALLWAY**!"

THE CENTER OF
THE BASE

Paulina had found the entrance to a long and narrow corridor that connected the trash room with the rest of the base.

The Thea Sisters went forward **CAREFULLY**, trying to make as little noise as possible.

"Stop here!" whispered Nicky suddenly, holding out her paw to keep her friends from moving.

"What is it?" whispered Colette.

Nicky pointed at a small flashing **RED LIGHT** at the top of the wall ahead.

"That's a camera . . ." Violet said quietly.

"Another **STEP** and we would've been caught for sure," Nicky said.

"Good catch," Collete said. "What do we

do now? We can't go that way!"

"Maybe we should go back to the elevator **tube** and get out," said Violet uncertainly.

"I doubt the buttons for that are in that room," Nicky said.

A camera!

"Give me **FIVE MINUTES**," Paulina squeaked. "If all goes well, we'll have another reason to thank our friend **Ren**!"

"What do you mean?" asked Pam.

"Let me see if I can get into the **network**," Paulina said, then took out her tablet and plugged in the flash drive that Ren had given them. She sat down and got to work.

The friends stayed as quiet as mice, waiting.

Finally, after a few minutes, Paulina raised her snout. With a big smile, she began a countdown: "Three, two, one . . ."

BZZZZZZZZZZZZZZZZZZZZZ

The red light on the camera on the wall turned off.

"But . . . was that you?" asked Colette, amazed.

"I used one of the programs that Ren wrote to connect the cameras and block them so that they stopped recording. For the next few hours, whoever watches them will just see the same still image!"

"Cheese on a stick!" Pam exclaimed.

"You and Ren are geniuses!"

"Shhh! Let's not ruin everything by yelling!" Violet scolded.

"Okay, sorry!" said Pam in a lower voice. "But they really are!"

Paulina *smiled* and put her things into her backpack. Then the Thea Sisters continued their walk toward the rest of the SECRET BASE.

HiDDEN iN FiRE

Now that they'd gotten past the security cameras, the Thea Sisters had to **FiND** Luke von Klawitz's headquarters.

It was silent, and the hallway they were walking down seemed to never end.

"Does anyone else feel like we've been walking in circles?" Nicky asked tensely.

"Don't worry," said Colette, squeezing her friend's paw. "I know that you don't like closed spaces, but you'll see — we'll get to the end soon!"

Violet stopped suddenly. "Nicky is right."

"Vi, don't make it **worse** than it already is!" Colette said.

Violet shook her snout. "No, I mean to

say that we are *actually* walking in circles! Do you see this round mark on the ground? I'm certain we've passed it before."

"Of course!" Paulina cried. "That's why we haven't yet gotten ANYWHERE ... We're just going around and around the same path!"

The mouselets stopped moving.

"So, what do we do now?!" squeaked Pam.

"I don't know ..." Colette sighed. "But I'm feeling really tired. Look at these BAGS under my eyes ..."

We've already passed through here!

I'm so tired!

She looked at her reflection in the **shiny** metal wall. "Wait a minute . . . mouselets!" she called.

"What is it, Coco?" Violet asked.

Colette *POINTED* to the wall. "The edges of the metal right here are uneven, as if . . ."

"It's a door!" Nicky cried, elated. She pushed, and the wall opened, revealing a passageway.

"Great Gorgonzola! You are marvemouse!" Pam cheered.

They went through the doorway, and the wall sealed closed behind them.

"Oh no . . . if Nicky felt claustrophobic in the hallway, I'm afraid it'll be even worse in here," Paulina said in a low voice, trying in vain to reopen the wall.

The Thea Sisters now found themselves in a **cramped** cell with stone walls. The room was dim, lit only by a small **FIREPIT**. On the opposite side, there was a small door.

Nicky tried to open it, but it was locked.

"What a strange place . . ." Colette said, shivering.

Paulina was examining every corner of the room.

"**Friends, I found something!** Here, there's writing on the ground . . ."

TO PROCEED, YOU CAN COUNT ON ONLY YOUR WIT AND THE ELEMENTS OF NATURE.

"It seems almost like a riddle . . ." Colette murmured.

"**For the love of cheese!** Klawitz made a labyrinth!" Pam said.

"Of course! It's like the professor's bunker!" Paulina exclaimed. "Remember? In her letter to Linda, she said that Jan von Klawitz had built a shelter that was a maze, to protect his precious collection . . ."

"So Luke was inspired by his ancestor and built a base to protect his treasures," Violet said.

"Which include Juliet's ring!" Colette added.

The Thea Sisters were sitting by the fire. The LIGHT from the weak flame danced on their snouts.

"**I have an idea.**" Pam broke the silence. "Paulina, can you pass me the backpack?"

Paulina gave it to her, and Pam pulled out a small CANTEEN.

"Your idea is to drink juice?" Nicky asked.

Pam shook her snout. "No, I want to try something." Then she poured the juice on the fire until it went out.

I want to try something!

"What are you doing?!" exclaimed Nicky. The room was pitch-dark.

Paulina took out her tablet from the backpack and used it as a flashlight. Pam was stomping on the **coals** of the firepit.

Then she bent down, blew away the remaining *ASH*, and poured out the last bit of juice.

Finally, she picked up a small object. "Here it is!" she said.

"What did you find?" asked Colette.

Pam held up a B°X. She opened it and found a key.

"How did you know that would be there?!" Colette cried.

"I used my wit!" Pam laughed. "And I thought about the only 'element of nature' in here, which was . . ."

"The **FIRE**!" Violet exclaimed. "Very clever!"

"Shall we try it?" Pam asked. Before waiting for a response, she went up to the door, put the **key** in the lock, and turned it.

"It works!" she cried.

And at that moment, a **TRAPDOOR** opened at her feet — and Pam disappeared.

AHEAD AT ANY COST

"Pam! Are you okay?!" the other Thea Sisters yelled into the hatch that had opened on the floor. It seemed to have been triggered by the key UNLOCKING the exit.

The mouselet had landed at the bottom of a pit that was BRIGHT and padded.

"Yes, give me a paw to come back up," said Pam.

Nicky leaned over to try and grab her friend's paw.

Violet said, "We should've known that Luke von Klawitz would put TRAPS into his maze! We'd better be careful."

After a few tries, Nicky said, "You're too far." For a few minutes, the mice tried to figure out a way to **PULL** their friend out of the pit, but they couldn't. They didn't have rope or anything similar, and no one else could go down into the pit without risking getting stuck in it, too.

"Don't worry, we'll turn back and go find help!" Paulina declared, turning to the hallway door.

"**NO WAY!**" ordered Pam from below. "We worked so hard to get here!"

"But . . . we can't leave you here!" Colette protested.

"Why not? It's comfortable . . . I could almost take a little **NAP**! Paulina, please pass me the energy bars I put in the left pocket of the backpack."

"That's not funny, Pam! We won't leave you!" Paulina said.

But Pam would not be swayed. She felt

that the most important thing was for her friends to *CONTINUE* on.

"Do you want to find the ring or not?" she asked.

Violet said, "Yes, of course, but —"

We'll come back to get her!

"No buts," Pam said. "I'm sure that *Aurora* would keep going!"

"You're right, Pam," Nicky said. "After all, the sooner we find the treasure, the sooner we can **come back** to get you."

So Paulina tossed the energy bars down, and the Thea Sisters left Pam.

"I don't like this even one

little bit," said Colette as she went through the UNLOCKED door.

Paulina put a paw around her shoulders. "Me, neither. But we can do this: We'll find the ring, and we will **COME RIGHT BACK**!"

A DEEP DIVE

Nicky, Paulina, Colette, and Violet continued on in the base to look for the **stolen** treasure.

The door that Pam had managed to unlock opened into a very different space.

"Everything is blue in here!" Paulina said, looking around in surprise.

The floor and walls of the **LARGE** room were the color of the sea, and every few seconds there was a wave of **sparkling** light. They could see a door on the opposite wall.

It took the mouselets a few moments to realize what was in the center of the room.

"It's a **pool**!" Colette said, amazed.

"Remember the inscription on the floor of the last room?" Violet said. "It talked about 'elements of nature' . . ."

"Cheese niblets! First there was fire . . . and here's water!" Paulina exclaimed.

Nicky approached the edge of the pool. "There's something shiny on the bottom. I bet it's the key to the door on the other side!" She immediately began to unlace her shoes.

I'm going to get it!

"You're not going to jump into the water, are you, Nicky?" Colette asked.

"Why not? It's the easiest way to get the **key**," Nicky replied.

Violet exclaimed, "Wait! This could be another **TRAP**!"

"Vi is right!" added Colette. "By now, we know that LUKE VON KLAWITZ has some tricks up his sleeve!"

But Nicky had decided. "If there is a TRAP, we'll find it when we try to open the DOOR to the next room, right? Now let me get the key — it's the first step to going forward! I'll be okay."

"Okay . . . but be very careful," Violet said.

"Don't worry, Vi. I'm a good swimmer! A pool like this doesn't scare me at all!" Nicky reassured her, winking.

Then she dove into the WATER.

"It's warm!" she said before fully immersing herself.

Her friends watched her swim to the bottom of the pool with a few decisive strokes. She reached the key and picked it up . . .

As soon as she grabbed it, the whole room LIT UP and the blue effect on the walls and floor disappeared. Everything turned white.

"WHAT'S HAPPENING?!" Colette squeaked.

"Look at the water!" Paulina yelled.

The water level in the pool was falling quickly, like it was being sucked down a drain.

"Hurry, Nicky! COME UP!" cried Colette, leaning toward her friend to help her out.

But it was too late. In a few seconds,

Nicky found herself on her paws at the bottom of a completely drained pool.

"You were right, friends," she said, dripping. "Now I can't **come back up** to you. Take this, though!" She gave the key a quick, precise toss, and Paulina caught it on the fly.

"No, no, no! I refuse to leave you behind, too!" Colette wailed, crossing her paws.

"If Pam can **wait**, I can wait, too," Nicky said, smiling. "I have a **dry** change of clothes in the backpack — can you leave those? Otherwise, it's warm, there's light, and I have faith in you: I know that you'll

Got it!

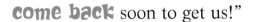
come back soon to get us!"

Paulina sighed. "I'm afraid there's nothing else to do. Coco, we've got to *KEEP GOING*."

I don't want to leave you!

Colette **gave in**. "Okay. But let's hurry to get to the end of this maze . . . I want to give that Klawitz a piece of my mind!"

A NEW CHALLENGE

Now only **three** of the Thea Sisters were left: Paulina, Colette, and Violet.

"Who knows if we're even getting closer to the **heart** of the base . . . With all these rooms, I've lost my sense of **direction**," Colette said.

Violet nodded. "Me too. But there are probably only two rooms left: one for AIR and another for **earth**!"

"Who knows what traps await us . . ." Colette sighed.

They unlocked the door using the key Nicky had retrieved, and **stepped** into a dimly lit room. It was mostly empty and seemed to have no doors.

"What are those?" asked Paulina. She approached four large wooden crates that each had another container on top.

Colette came over. "They look like big flowerpots . . ." She tried to look in them but couldn't tell if anything was there. "It's too **DARK**!"

Violet had gone toward the opposite wall. "Squeak! There's something written here!"

Her friends joined her, and together they read the words that flickered on a dimly lit panel:

Together I'm solid,
I'm small when I break down,
Roots sink into me,
Water shapes me.
If you know what I am,
Press the buttons in the right order
And bring light to this cave.

But remember:
You may only be wrong once
or you'll stay here forever.

"Earth . . ." whispered Violet. "This is the room for **earth**!"

"There are buttons here, over each container!" Paulina said.

Colette frowned, stressed. "**BRIE ON A BAGUETTE!** We have to be careful — if we make more than one mistake, we'll get stuck in here and never free our friends!"

The mouselets studied the riddle in *silence*.

"Well, we know the **RIDDLE** is about earth, even if not all the details are clear," Violet said.

"And we know we need to press the **buttons** in a certain order to reveal the exit," Paulina added.

"Let's try to look at what is in each container," Violet suggested.

Paulina took her tablet out of her bag. "I'll

use this for LIGHT . . . oh no!"

"What's wrong?" Colette asked.

"The battery's dead!" Paulina said.

"Cheddar chunks! Okay . . . we'll figure this out . . ." Violet murmured. "We have to put our paws in the containers!"

"I knew it was useless to get a manicure before traveling," Colette said, sighing as she stuck her paw into the first pot. "It feels like there's sand in here!"

Violet exclaimed, "Aha! 'I'm small when I break down': sand is described in the second line of the riddle. So we'll need to press the button above it second!"

Paulina put her paw into another pot and immediately pulled it out again, saying, "Blech! That feels like mud!"

"'Water shapes me': into mud!" Colette said. "So that's the fourth button."

Violet **dipped** her paw into the third pot. "This is full of **stones** . . . which are 'solid' like the first line of the riddle!"

Soil!

"And I'm sure that in this last one, there's . . . **SOIL**!" Paulina said, putting her paw in and pulling out dirt. "Which 'roots sink into'!"

Now the mouselets knew the right order to push the **buttons**.

Violet reread the riddle. "'Together I'm solid': That's the rock, so **FIRST** we press the button above the stones."

"Done!" said Colette. An ORANGE LIGHT came on above it.

Violet continued. "'I'm small when I break down' . . ."

"Sand!" Paulina said, pressing the button above the sand container, which activated a YELLOW LIGHT.

"Next is 'Roots sink into me': soil!" Violet said.

Colette pressed that button, making a GREEN LIGHT come on.

"And to finish, 'Water shapes' —"

Before Violet could finish squeaking, Paulina pushed the button above the pot full of mud.

A RED LIGHT came on above that, and a loud buzzer started blaring.

"**We did it!**" Colette cheered. "Now we just —"

Suddenly, the floor began to vibrate and then a hidden **TRAPDOOR** in front of the last pot sprang open.

"That must be the exit! Hurry!" Paulina said, and pushed Colette, who **slipped down** through the trapdoor.

Violet followed her, but Paulina ran over to grab her tablet from the corner of the room.

She rushed back . . . but it was too late. The door had shut with a CLICK.

It's closed . . .

A POWERFUL OBSTACLE

Colette and Violet slid down a short **slide** that connected to the trapdoor, and emerged in a long hallway.

"Where's Paulina?" Colette asked, *worried*.

Paulina?

"The trapdoor closed too soon," Violet said sadly. "Paulina is stuck in the earth room."

"This is too much!" Colette was angry. "First Pam, then Nicky, now Paulina . . . I don't like it!"

"Snout up, Coco," Violet said, giving her a hug. "You'll see — we'll get the ring soon, and then we'll rescue our friends right after. Remember what Aurora wrote in her letters?"

"True strength lies in a kind heart," Colette murmured, though a small tear rolled down her snout. "But without all my friends, I don't feel brave . . ."

"I know," Violet agreed. "But we have to stay strong and face this last test. This must be the room of AIR, the last of the four elements of nature . . ."

"In fact, there's nothing in here other than air!" Colette said with a weak smile.

"And the door," added her friend, pointing at the large METAL DOOR at the other end of the hallway.

The two girls reached the exit in a few steps. Violet said, "That seemed too easy . . ."

"Let's try to open it! I want to finish this treasure hunt and go get our friends as soon as possible!" Colette grabbed the handle and pulled the door firmly. It opened a few inches — but then a very strong GUST OF WIND pushed it closed.

"But . . . what just happened?!"

"As soon as you started opening the door, an air vent in the wall opened and blasted a VERY POWERFUL air current," Violet explained. "Let's try it together!"

The two friends pulled on the door

together. Again, as soon as it opened a crack, a wind like a **HURRICANE** started. It pushed the door closed once more, and made the mouselets lose their balance.

"If this keeps happening, we'll **NEVER** get out!" Violet grunted. "Luke von Klawitz has an evil mind!"

"That's true . . . there are two of us!" Colette said, smiling. "Of course, it would have been better if there were five of us: **All**

together, we could have opened this door with no problem! But I think the two of us can still do it."

"How?"

"Here's my idea: I'll hold the door open by wedging my arms and legs against the frame. Then you go through under my leg!" Colette proposed.

Violet thought about it for a second. "But how will **YOU** get out?"

"You can do the same thing from the other side," Colette suggested.

"Okay — let's try it!"

Together, the mice pulled on the door handle. As soon as the **wind** rose, Colette stuck her foot between the door and its frame.

"Go as fast as you can! I don't know how long I can hold this . . . *The wind is getting*

stronger!" she said as the gusts whipped her fur.

Violet **CRAWLED** through. "Okay, now I'll try to hold it . . ."

But the force of the wind was increasing. The friends tried their best, but in the end, they couldn't keep the **DOOR** open.

Colette yelled, "**You go on! We're all with you!**"

Then she gave in to the wind and let the door go. It slammed shut.

Violet found herself **ALONE**.

WHAT TiME iS iT?

For the first time in a long time, Luke von Klawitz felt satisfied. Finally, he had made one of the Seven Treasures of the World his own, beating out the five annoying mouselets who were following the pawsteps of Aurora Beatrix Lane. The Ring of True Love that his henchmice had brought him was now safely in his **TREASURE ROOM** among the other precious objects in his collection.

He opened the notebook and leafed through it. "It's time for a new mission . . . What will the next treasure be?"

After a few minutes, he raised his snout from the pages.

Something had disturbed him, but he didn't know what.

He jumped up and went to the wall-sized MONITOR that tracked the activity of everything related to LVK, twenty-four hours a day.

Some windows on-screen reported data and research. Others showed the video footage of the inside and outside of the BASE.

Luke studied the surveillance video in silence.

"It's too quiet," Luke said. "I don't like it . . ."

Camera 3 showed an empty room where

he could see the profile of a super-modern helicopter.

Camera **9** showed the blue **water** room with a full pool.

Camera **12** showed the **TREASURE ROOM**, where the display cases were all in place.

Camera **15** showed a corner of a hallway with a digital clock that read 1:00.

Luke checked his watch: **It was 4:15**.

"Aha! My instinct is never wrong . . . It even notices a **BROKEN** clock!" Luke laughed, then turned on a tablet and sent a message to Cassidy.

With a sigh, Luke sat down again on his **large** couch and continued reading from Jan von Klawitz's notebook, looking for details that could put him on the trail of a **new treasure**.

Broken clock in hallway 5.
This carelessness is unacceptable.

While he read, he didn't notice that something set off the motion detector in his most precious and protected space: the treasure room.

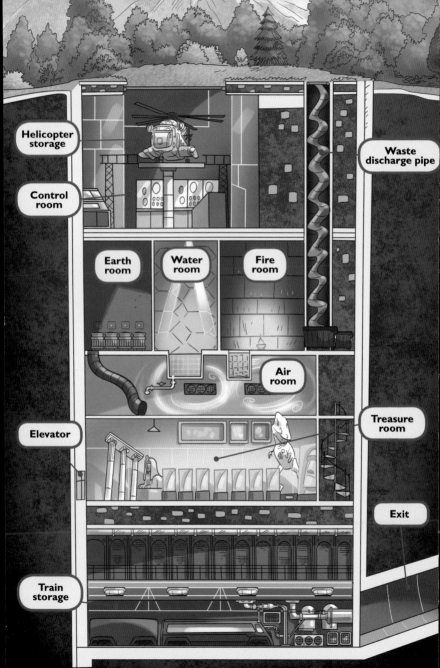

Helicopter storage

Control room

Waste discharge pipe

Earth room

Water room

Fire room

Air room

Treasure room

Elevator

Exit

Train storage

iN THE TREASURE ROOM

Violet took a deep breath. She was alone, but she could do this. She walked **FORWARD**.

By now, Klawitz's base was clear in her mind. She and her friends had accidentally *entered* the bunker through a long tube for waste removal. From there, they passed through the hallway with the security **camera**, and Paulina had been able to **block** all the videos at once. Then they'd gone into the four rooms based on the elements of nature . . .

There was the **FIRE** room, where Pam had found the key to its exit but ended up

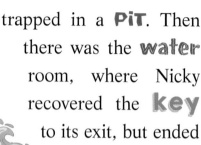

trapped in a **PiT**. Then there was the **water** room, where Nicky recovered the **key** to its exit, but ended up trapped in an empty pool. Then there was the **earth** room, where Paulina had ended up trapped, leaving just Violet and Colette to go forward. And then there was the **AIR** room, which was difficult to get out of — and Colette ended up trapped inside to allow Violet to keep going.

Now Violet was by herself. She'd overcome the challenges of the FOUR ELEMENTS, and she felt that she was finally close to their goal: finding the *Ring of True Love*. Of course, then she had to help her friends escape, and they all 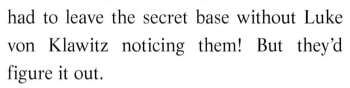 had to leave the secret base without Luke von Klawitz noticing them! But they'd figure it out.

Outside the air room, Violet found herself in a hallway with a spiral staircase going downward. She went down the stairs and found a closed sliding door, similar to that of an elevator.

The mouselet took a decisive step forward, and the door in front of her **OPENED**.

"Oh!" Violet said aloud, unable to hold in her **amazement**.

She was at the entrance to a **LARGE**

ROOM that was completely different from what she'd seen so far. It was like a gallery in a museum!

She didn't know where to look — magnificent works of **art** filled every corner.

Violet saw a large area dedicated to **ancient art**. There were beautiful statues; a reassembled portico with tall marble **COLUMNS**; an entire imposing entrance to a temple that was perfectly reconstructed; and **beautiful**, intact Greek and Roman jars.

In another area of the room, Violet admired elegant antique furniture — including a canopy bed that probably belonged to a princess — and large paintings by **famouse artists** of the past.

Two large dinosaur skeletons stood in a corner next to some medieval armor. Another corner of the room was occupied by sparkling crowns and other gold objects studded with precious stones . . .

But what really caught Violet's eye were the SEVEN DISPLAY CASES in the center of the room.

"These must be for the seven treasures Aurora was looking for," she thought. Six were empty. In the seventh, a magnificent ruby ring sparkled.

"Juliet's ring . . ." she whispered excitedly. "We did it!"

Without thinking, Violet reached her paw

to the glass and take the ring.

Immediately, a loud alarm started blaring, followed by a robotic voice:

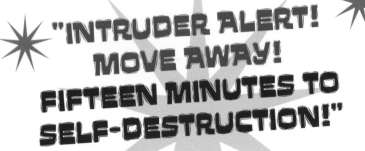

"INTRUDER ALERT! MOVE AWAY! FIFTEEN MINUTES TO SELF-DESTRUCTION!"

AN UNEXPECTED OFFER

With her heart in her throat, she closed the case without taking the ring, hoping to stop the alarm. But it did not stop. In fact, she heard another deep rumble in addition to the siren.

It took Violet a few seconds to realize that it was an ELEVATOR coming to the hall she was in.

BINNNG!

The door **OPENED**, and Luke von Klawitz appeared in front of her.

Violet had already met the rat who had tried to **STOP** the Thea Sisters, but she'd never seen him looking so distressed.

When he saw her, though, the head of LVK regained his usual **EVIL** smile.

"So it's you, little mouseling . . . I should have known," he said.

"I — w-we . . ." Violet babbled, a little afraid to find herself face-to-face with Klawitz all alone.

Luke sighed. "Of course. Now it's up to me to solve the problem . . ."

"You've already done more than enough!" Violet cried, suddenly finding her courage. "This place is full of stolen art, isn't it?"

"Stolen?" Luke snickered. "It's my private collection . . . put together piece by piece by generations of **KLAWITZ** mice, by any means we could."

"That's not true, you stole these. They deserve to be displayed in public mouseums, not hidden underground!" Violet protested.

"You're smart," Luke replied. "Do you think any mouseum would take better care of these **masterpieces**? No one loves them more than me!"

The flash of pure greed that sparkled in Klawitz's eyes made Violet STEP BACK.

"You were going to take the *Treasure of True Love*, weren't you?" Luke boomed.

"I must . . . we must take it!" Violet exclaimed. "You have no right to keep it here. It doesn't belong to you. It doesn't belong to anymouse! My friends and I came to Alaska

TO CARRY OUT AURORA'S MISSION . . ."

Luke von Klawitz was silent for an instant, before smiling and saying, "You're skilled.

No ordinary mouse could have gotten into this **bunker**, through the maze, and all the way to the treasure room . . ."

"Well, I didn't do it all on my own, I had help," Violet said, trying to distract him while she came up with a plan.

"Why do you **insist** on stealing the treasure? It doesn't make sense. Leave them for everyone to enjoy, and —"

Klawitz interrupted her with a wave of his paw. "That's enough, little rat. Do you hear that alarm? It means the entire

Give me the ring!

I have an idea . . .

base is going to **self-destruct**. There's no time to waste!"

Violet turned as pale as mozzarella. "My . . . my friends . . . I have to go back for them. They're all trapped . . ."

"Forget those **BRATS**! You're the only one who managed to get here! You used your friends to get here. And in doing so, you demonstrated true **TALENT** . . . so much that I have an offer for you."

"**An . . . offer?!**" Violet repeated.

Luke von Klawitz nodded. "Leave your friends and become my **partner**. For some time now, I've been looking for someone at my level who will help me find **new riches** and make my collection the most important and valuable in the world! No one on my team is quite as smart as you."

"Wh-what?!" Violet stuttered, too shocked

to respond.

"If you accept, we can divide everything," Luke went on. "Then you, too, will understand what it means to have priceless **artwork** all to yourself, to admire anytime you want. You could own a real painting by Van Gogh, or dip your paws into a bowl of Aztec gold coins. Or wear a rare pearl necklace, or the tiara of a famous empress . . ."

Luke took a sparkly tiara out of a jewelry box, then came over and placed it on Violet's head. He turned her toward an *elegant* mirror with a golden frame.

"Forget your friends," he said. "You can keep this tiara and become as **rich** as a queen. What do you say?"

THE POWER OF FRIENDSHIP

"I don't like what I see at all," Violet said, taking the precious tiara off her head and placing it on a chair.

"The only way I got here," she continued, facing Klawitz and looking at him directly in the eyes, "was thanks to the power of friendship. And that is my true treasure!"

"Are you going to turn your back on unbelievable riches?" Luke asked, gesturing at the room full of masterpieces.

Violet nodded. "What matters to me most is what's in the other rooms: four friends who are like SISTERS to me. There are no riches or treasures in the whole world that could ever make me abandon them!"

"You're even more naïve than I thought," Luke said in a **SHARP** tone. "Too bad for you."

He went to leave.

Violet realized that the only **hope** she and her friends had of saving themselves would disappear with him. She had to stop him.

"You can't be okay with losing all these treasures!" she squeaked.

Luke turned to her and **laughed**.

"You think I'd risk them? These works of art won't be destroyed: The rest of the base will collapse, but this room will remain safe and closed off. The **treasures** will be safe . . . unlike you and your friends!

HA, HA, HA, HA, HA, HA, HA!"

At that, he scurried into the elevator and disappeared. His laughter echoed as the elevator took him upward.

Violet heard a new message from the alarm:

"TEN MINUTES TO SELF-DESTRUCTION!"

The mouselet took a deep breath. She had very little time. She took the *Treasure of True Love* and then ran to the elevator and pressed the call button.

After a few seconds, the doors **OPENED** and Violet got in. There were four buttons to choose from, each with a different icon. "But where should I go?" Violet asked herself, panic tightening her throat.

She took a deep breath and studied the buttons. The gold crown was iLLUMiNaTeD, so that must be where the elevator was currently: the treasure room.

The top floor, where KLaWitZ had gone, had a helicopter on the button. It was probably an escape route . . . but she couldn't **PUSH** it. It needed a key to activate it.

Her friends were still nearby, locked in each of the four element rooms . . . how could she get them out?

Violet **STARED** at the two remaining buttons: The bottom button had a **TRAIN** on it, and the button under the helicopter showed a computer monitor.

"Jumping gerbils! The control room!" she realized, and pushed it at once.

The elevator went **UP**. A moment later, the doors opened, and the alarm sounded louder than ever:

"EIGHT MINUTES TO SELF-DESTRUCTION!"

Violet shuddered. But she saw that she'd been right: The room she was now in was the command center for the base. There was an enormouse SCREEN covered in flashing alerts, and in front of it were keyboards, microphones, and various controls, as well as a **LARGE** dark chair.

"Okay, let's see . . . I have to stop the self-destruction of the base before it's too late!" Violet said, approaching the **control panel**.

I must do it!

COUNTDOWN

As Violet watched, four **WINDOWS** on the monitor seemed to reset.

"The cameras that Paulina had blocked must be back on," Violet whispered. She looked closely at one **SCREEN** and saw Luke von Klawitz climbing onto a helicopter, ready to **escape**.

After a few seconds, the platform the helicopter was on began to rise up, and the ceiling opened. Soon the aircraft was out of the camera's view.

The window for the next camera showed something that made her **wince**: Nicky was sitting at the bottom of the empty pool in the water room, looking tense.

"Don't worry, sister! I'll save you!" Violet murmured.

But how?

There were hundreds of BUTTONS

on the keyboard in front of her. Violet tried to activate a small tablet connected to the panel, but it needed a password.

"SIX MINUTES TO SELF-DESTRUCTION!"

"Oh no . . . now what do I do?!" Violet said, panicking.

The alarm blared **LOUDER AND LOUDER**, and a clock on the wall was counting down the seconds of the few minutes remaining.

Violet wanted to **CRY**.

The base would soon be destroyed, her friends were trapped, and . . .

"**Stay calm!** Take a nice, deep breath!"

"CHEESE AND CRACKERS, you can do it, sister!"

"Have faith in yourself!"

"Find the right button!"

The voices of her friends rang louder than the ALARM, as if the Thea Sisters were all there together in the control room.

Colette urging her to be calm, Pam pumping her up, Paulina keeping faith in her, and Nicky suggesting a next step to take . . . Their words, their faces, and their love were so alive in her heart that she felt the heat, stronger than anything.

"You're right, friends! I can do it!" Violet said aloud.

She CONCENTRATED on the control panel and noticed a button that she hadn't seen before. It was round and had four small symbols around it: a FLAME, a water drop, a STONE, and a vortex of air.

"The elements of nature!" Violet exclaimed, and pressed it.

On the water room screen, she saw that

a ladder had dropped down into the pool. Nicky immediately climbed it and escaped through a trapdoor that had opened wide above her!

Then she saw Pam appear on the screen — she must have gotten out of the pit and was running in from the fire room. Soon the four mice had escaped their traps, and they all ended up in the treasure room.

As soon as the elevator doors opened, tears came to her eyes: All her best friends were there!

"Vi!" Colette cried, running to hug her. *"You did it! You saved us!"*

The friends held one another in a hug.

Friends!

"I missed you, sisters!" Pam said.

But a message interrupted their reunion:

"FOUR MINUTES TO SELF-DESTRUCTION!"

"Self-destruction?!" Colette shrieked. "Does that mean what I think it does?!"

Violet took her by the paw. "We have to hurry. Follow me!"

THE LAST SECOND

Violet had a plan.

Klawitz had used the helicopter on the top floor to **escape**, but the Thea Sisters couldn't get there. However, there was still one button in the elevator that Violet had not pressed: the train.

"I think there's a way out of here **below us**," she said as they all got into the elevator.

She pressed the lowest button. The elevator went **DOWN** and stopped at the deepest level of the base.

"Sweet Swiss on a stick! That's a train!" Pam exclaimed.

In the glow of a flickering

fluorescent light, they could see that they were at the mouth of a large tunnel that was almost completely filled by what seemed to be a **FREIGHT TRAIN**.

"How on earth did a train get down here?!" asked Colette.

"Klawitz probably used it to bring whatever he needed **INSIDE** the base," Paulina guessed.

"Like construction materials or electronics," Nicky added, pointing at a sack of lime and a wheelbarrow cluttered with cables nearby.

"And treasures!" Violet said. "I wondered how he was able to traNSport those huge pieces of the temple, enormouse furniture, and statues as tall as —"

"THREE MINUTES TO SELF-DESTRUCTION!"

"Oh no! Pam, can you get this thing started?" Colette squeaked, pointing at the train.

"I'll try my best! Follow me!" Pam said.

In a moment, the mouselets jumped aboard and entered the train's cab. Pam sat in front of an old-fashioned **control**

Hmmm...let's see...

panel that was full of levers, buttons, and ᴛɪɴʏ writing that was hard to read.

"This won't be easy . . ." Pam muttered, staring at the controls.

"Do you want us to give you a paw?" Paulina offered. She bent over the panel, but was soon bewildered. "**What?!** Aren't there digital controls?"

"No, this is an old train . . ." Pam said.

"Wait! There's a **bar** in front, blocking the tracks!" Nicky yelled, leaning out the cab door. "I'm going to go move it!"

"I'm coming with you!" Paulina called, and leaped down with her friend.

"TWO MINUTES TO SELF-DESTRUCTION!"

Pam was motionless, staring at the buttons.

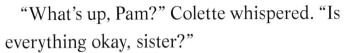

"What's up, Pam?" Colette whispered. "Is everything okay, sister?"

"**INITIATE LEVER!**" Pam said.

"Huh?"

Pam smiled and explained, "I remembered that when I was a mouseling, my dad took me to see a train operator at work. If I'm not mistaken, all we have to do is push this **button** . . ."

She pulled it, but the train didn't start.

"Hang on!" Violet shouted. "We need **ELECTRICITY**!"

She ran to the cab door and called out to Nicky and Paulina, who had just finished moving the bar, "We need to turn on the **POWER** . . . but be careful!"

"Okay!" Nicky squeaked, and went up to the panel with Paulina. They pressed a button to turn the electricity on.

"ONE MINUTE TO SELF-DESTRUCTION!"

Lights appeared on the train's control panel, and Pam yelled, "**WE'VE GOT IT!**"

Nicky and Paulina jumped back on board just as Pam pushed the button.

"THIRTY SECONDS TO SELF-DESTRUCTION!"

"Go, go, go!" Pam squeaked. Her friends huddled around her.

The train started slowly along the track, which wound through the darkness of the tunnel and went uphill.

"Ten . . . Nine . . . Eight . . ."

As the train picked up *SPEED* and chugged through the tunnel, they stopped being able to hear the countdown . . . and soon emerged into the open air of **ALASKA**!

THE FINAL SURPRISE

A moose raised its head and stared in amazement at the strange, large METAL MACHINE going by not far from it. Then it shook its head, gave a snort, and trotted away.

"And now . . . stop, now, yes, stop, stop, stop!" Pam squeaked in the cab of the **TRAIN** as she pushed down the brake lever. They came to a **Halt** near a group of trees. They'd made it out! **"YOU WERE FABUMOUSE!"**

Colette exclaimed, hugging her friend.

"No . . . *we* were fabumouse!" Pam said. "It was truly teamwork!"

Paulina nodded. "I have to admit, I was scared that this time, we couldn't do it. Luke von Klawitz's headquarters were one big trap!"

"I also got especially nervous when I heard the '**four minutes to self-destruction**' announcement!" Violet said.

Nicky added a bit tensely, "I'd like to squeak about what happened, but . . . can we get off this thing first?!"

The other Thea Sisters burst out laughing.

"Of course, Nicky," said Violet. "Let's go . . . I think we all want to be **outdoors** after so much time locked in that bunker!"

The mouselets got off the **TRAIN** and

stretched. Nicky jogged around a bit, Paulina and Colette did some yoga stretches, Violet sat on a rock and took deep, **calming** breaths with her eyes closed, and Pam bent over some bushes.

"Pam, what are you doing?" Colette asked.

"I'm having a **snack**!" Pam responded.

"Of . . . leaves?!"

"No, of these!" Pam said with a big smile, opening her paw. It was full of juicy **raspberries** that she'd just picked.

"Oh, wow . . . I think I'll join you!" Colette giggled.

A moment later, Pam asked, "So, what do we do now?"

"The first thing we need to do is tell the local authorities — I'm sure they didn't know about the existence of the underground base here, even if it is ruined. Maybe they can recover the treasures stolen by Luke von Klawitz . . ." Violet began.

Paulina nodded. "They can also take care of moving this train . . . We certainly can't leave it here in the middle of nature!"

"Okay, let's go back to the car, and we'll figure everything out!" concluded Colette.

As they walked, Paulina reflected, "It was a great adventure, wasn't it? I think Aurora would be proud of us!"

Raspberries!

How delicious!

"Even if we weren't able to recover the treasure this time, we did everything possible," Colette said.

"You're wrong!" Violet said, stopping in her tracks.

"But, Vi," Nicky said. "What more could we have done? We tried our hardest, and that counts for a lot . . ."

Violet gave them a mysterious smile and put a paw in her pocket.

The friends began to understand. "Are you saying . . ." Colette murmured.

Violet pulled out her closed paw and slowly opened it.

"Juliet's ring!" Paulina shrieked. The enormouse ruby sparkled in the sunlight.

"But . . . how did you do it?!" asked Pam.

Violet explained, "I took it right before LEAVING the treasure room when I went

to try to free you. Can you believe that before he ran away, Klawitz came to me and offered me half his **riches** if I became his partner in crime?!"

"What?!" Pam squeaked. "For the love of cheese, what did you say to him?!"

"I told him I already had the greatest treasure in the world: true friendship!"

The Thea Sisters hugged one another, happy to be done with their mission — and to have rescued another of the seven very precious **treasures** found almost a century before by the brave archaeologist *Aurora Beatrix Lane.*

This adventure had been full of ups and downs, but it ended in the best of ways:

a lost treasure found and a stronger friendship than ever!

Thea Stilton

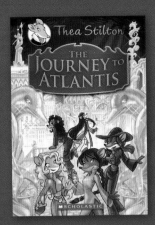

Secret Fairies

Don't miss any of these exciting series featuring the Thea Sisters!

Treasure Seekers

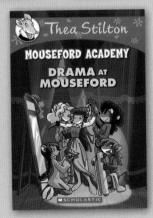

Mouseford Academy

Don't miss any of these exciting Thea Sisters adventures!

Thea Stilton and the Dragon's Code

Thea Stilton and the Mountain of Fire

Thea Stilton and the Ghost of the Shipwreck

Thea Stilton and the Secret City

Thea Stilton and the Mystery in Paris

Thea Stilton and the Cherry Blossom Adventure

Thea Stilton and the Star Castaways

Thea Stilton: Big Trouble in the Big Apple

Thea Stilton and the Ice Treasure

Thea Stilton and the Secret of the Old Castle

Thea Stilton and the Blue Scarab Hunt

Thea Stilton and the Prince's Emerald

Thea Stilton and the Mystery on the Orient Express

Thea Stilton and the Dancing Shadows

Thea Stilton and the Legend of the Fire Flowers

Thea Stilton and the Spanish Dance Mission

**Thea Stilton and the
Journey to the Lion's Den**

**Thea Stilton and the
Great Tulip Heist**

**Thea Stilton and the
Chocolate Sabotage**

**Thea Stilton and the
Missing Myth**

**Thea Stilton and the
Lost Letters**

**Thea Stilton and the
Tropical Treasure**

**Thea Stilton and the
Hollywood Hoax**

**Thea Stilton and the
Madagascar Madness**

**Thea Stilton and the
Frozen Fiasco**

**Thea Stilton and the
Venice Masquerade**

**Thea Stilton and the
Niagara Splash**

**Thea Stilton and the
Riddle of the Ruins**

**Thea Stilton and the
Phantom of the Orchestra**

**Thea Stilton and the
Black Forest Burglary**

**Thea Stilton and the
Race for the Gold**

**Thea Stilton and the
Rainforest Rescue**

**Thea Stilton and the
American Dream**

Check out these very special editions!

THE JOURNEY TO ATLANTIS   **THE SECRET OF THE FAIRIES**   **THE SECRET OF THE SNOW**   **THE CLOUD CASTLE**   **THE TREASURE OF THE SEA**

THE LAND OF FLOWERS   **THE SECRET OF THE CRYSTAL FAIRIES**   **THE DANCE OF THE STAR FAIRIES**   **THE MAGIC OF THE MIRROR**

THE JOURNEY THROUGH TIME   **BACK IN TIME**   **THE RACE AGAINST TIME**   **LOST IN TIME**

NO TIME TO LOSE   **THE TEST OF TIME**   **TIME WARP**   **OUT OF TIME**

Don't miss any of my adventures in the Kingdom of Fantasy!

THE KINGDOM OF FANTASY

THE QUEST FOR PARADISE:
THE RETURN TO THE KINGDOM OF FANTASY

THE AMAZING VOYAGE:
THE THIRD ADVENTURE IN THE KINGDOM OF FANTASY

THE DRAGON PROPHECY:
THE FOURTH ADVENTURE IN THE KINGDOM OF FANTASY

THE VOLCANO OF FIRE:
THE FIFTH ADVENTURE IN THE KINGDOM OF FANTASY

THE SEARCH FOR TREASURE:
THE SIXTH ADVENTURE IN THE KINGDOM OF FANTASY

THE ENCHANTED CHARMS:
THE SEVENTH ADVENTURE IN THE KINGDOM OF FANTASY

THE PHOENIX OF DESTINY:
AN EPIC KINGDOM OF FANTASY ADVENTURE

THE HOUR OF MAGIC:
THE EIGHTH ADVENTURE IN THE KINGDOM OF FANTASY

THE WIZARD'S WAND:
THE NINTH ADVENTURE IN THE KINGDOM OF FANTASY

THE SHIP OF SECRETS:
THE TENTH ADVENTURE IN THE KINGDOM OF FANTASY

THE DRAGON OF FORTUNE:
AN EPIC KINGDOM OF FANTASY ADVENTURE

THE GUARDIAN OF THE REALM:
THE ELEVENTH ADVENTURE IN THE KINGDOM OF FANTASY

THE ISLAND OF DRAGONS:
THE TWELFTH ADVENTURE IN THE KINGDOM OF FANTASY

THE BATTLE FOR THE CRYSTAL CASTLE:
THE THIRTEENTH ADVENTURE IN THE KINGDOM OF FANTASY

Don't miss a single fabumouse adventure!

Up Next:

You've never seen
Geronimo Stilton like this before!

Get your paws on the all-new

Geronimo Stilton

graphic novels. You've gouda* have them!

*Gouda is
a type
of cheese.